Table of Contents

Hidden
Florella Grant

This is a work of fiction. Names, characters, places, and incidents are products of the author's imagination or are used fictitiously and should not be construed as real.

Any resemblance to actual events, locales, organizations or persons, living or dead, is entirely coincidental.

Hidden: One title. Endless possibilities.

From sci-fi to romance, fantasy to cozy mystery & many more, the Hidden Project has something for everyone. Each author has taken the same title, and put their own spin on the story, leading to a wide range of stories in a variety of genres.

You can check out all the books in the Hidden Project here: www.HiddenReader.com[1]

Or join us on Facebook http://www.facebook.com/hiddenreader[2] or subscribe to our newsletter http://eepurl.com/cHr3Q1

---

1.   http://l.facebook.com/

l.php?u=http%3A%2F%2Fwww.HiddenReader.com%2F&h=ATPwAiSI7QOFuKJZC88cvmrdRm

MrFB-ntluMJKihDrK6P01UDkuIKdbFpc35rWGN942EvNbYeDs05RE65oeyWSPKorcIdxCkJWpi

jugyjB69UxuObHayozWJj-LduE2CJ0g

2.   https://www.facebook.com/hiddenreader

Chapter 1

A TEAR RAN DOWN CASSANDRA'S cheek as her mother knelt to kiss her. "Run, Cassandra, run." The last images of her mother ran clearly through Cassandra Frame's mind. "Run," she pleaded again. Cassandra stood still, shook her head and squeezed her mother's hand. "I'll always love you," her mother whispered. Cassandra took off as fast as her tiny feet could run.

A gunshot stopped Cassandra in her tracks. "Mommy," she screamed, and made a beeline to return to her mother's side. A man stepped out of the shadows and pulled her away from the light. "Mommy," she cried again.

The man squatted down beside her and covered her mouth. She didn't feel he was dangerous, somehow, she knew he was there to help her. "Stay back here and be quiet," he warned. Cassandra shook her head and attempted to pass him. He held her back and wiped a tear from her eye with his thumb. Cassandra looked in to his electric blue eyes and they seemed to soothe her. She took a deep breath and nodded in agreement. "I'll be back," he said. "I promise."

The memory of her mother's death caused Cassandra's eyes to pop open and she realized the danger that surrounded her. A blinding beam of light shone through a broken window and her eyes flinched. She looked around and tried to figure out where she was. The room was small and dirty, tiny particles of dust danced around in the sunray, and a musky scent filled the air.

Cassandra attempted to sit up, but found her wrists and ankles tied. The more she tried to move them, the more the rope dug into her skin. A wad of clothe was shoved into her mouth, as much as Cassandra tried to push it out with her tongue, the rag wouldn't budge. She squirmed and almost fell off the dingy bedding she laid on. Her vision blurred, and her head weighed more than she ever remembered. Cassandra blinked to clear her eyes. A stranger stepped toward her from the darkened corner of the room, and she wondered why she didn't notice him before.

She tried to scream, but her cries were muffled by the rag. The stranger approached as Cassandra wiggled her way back against the wall. "I'm going to take this out of your mouth," he told her. "If you scream, I'll shove another needle in your ass." His words confirmed what Cassandra thought, she'd been drugged.

He leaned close to Cassandra as he reached for the knot behind her head and she couldn't help but look in his pools of blue. She blinked again, they couldn't be as blue as the eyes in her dream. His breath burned into her skin as he fumbled with the knot. As she looked at him, something called out to her. There was something other than his eyes that mesmerized her. As the man's brawny body inched closer to her, she noticed his squared jaw and dark brown crew cut. Cassandra looked in his eyes and felt her soul being pierced. She tore her gaze away from his eyes and ignored the rising temperature of her body as he leaned back and pulled the rag with him.

Her tongue felt like sandpaper scraping her lips. "Water?" She begged. Cassandra's throat and dry mouth burned as she spoke.

The stranger walked to the other side of the room and came back with a bottle and placed it in her hands. Cassandra attempted to bring it to her mouth, but her tied hands shook and water spilled out onto her chest. Finally, she placed the opening in her mouth and she took a sip. Her throat closed, and the liquid fell down her chin. The stranger watched but didn't help. She tried again. Water moistened her lips but stung like a bitch as she swallowed.

"Who are you?" Cassandra asked after drinking half the bottle. The stranger untied her wrists and ankles but didn't reply. She considered running for help, but every attempt to move failed. Her jelly-like body fell back on the bed as the room spun around her.

The mattress smelled of urine, but Cassandra was too tired to care. She curled into a ball and went back to sleep. "*There wasn't a man there," she heard her therapist yell at her.*

Cassandra woke but kept her eyes closed as she thought about all the therapy sessions she attended throughout her lifetime. The doctor, and her father, told her many times that the man she thought she saw the night her mother died did not exist. Cassandra knew he did and he had eyes that matched her abductor's.

When she opened her eyes, the room was dark except for a small lamp coming from the other side. Cassandra looked around and prayed she'd find a way to escape. The stranger slept slouched on a chair, she listened closely to his shallow breathing and when she heard him begin to snore, she knew she needed to make a move. She sat up on the makeshift bed and inched toward the edge. Cassandra slid her feet over the side to stand up but woke the stranger in the process.

"Where do you think you're going?" His husky voice scared the crap out of her and she quickly pushed herself back onto the mattress until her head hit the wall behind her. He leaned forward in his chair and barked again. "I said, where the fuck do you think you're going?"

Tears stung Cassandra's eyes. "I need to use the bathroom," she mumbled.

"Do you see one?"

Cassandra's eyes adjusted to the darkness and she looked around. There was a door opposite of her bedding, but it was the only one which she assumed was the entrance to the room, not a bathroom. Her eyes scanned a large bucket and she prayed it wasn't what she would have to use to relieve herself. The thought alone made her forget she had to go.

She pulled her knees up to her chest and rocked back and forth. Cassandra sobbed but tried not to let him hear. "What do you want from me?" She found the courage to ask.

"Shut up. And don't ask questions," he warned.

She stayed quiet for a moment but couldn't help but try and talk her way out of danger. "If it's money you want, my father—"

The stranger threw a mason jar across the room and it shattered. "I don't want shit from your father," he screamed.

Cassandra's pulse raced. If he didn't want money, what did he want?

"Who are you?" Cassandra asked.

He jumped up from his seat and stormed toward her. Cassandra lowered her head toward her knees but felt his presence near her. He reached over and slowly traced her jawline with his finger. Chills went up her spine as thoughts of him forcing himself on her entered her mind. "Please don't," she pleaded.

"Please don't what?" He stopped touching her face but didn't leave her side.

Cassandra gulped then answered. "Don't touch me." She crossed her arm over her ripped t-shirt and hid her breasts from him.

The stranger burst out in laughter. "Don't worry, raping isn't my style." Cassandra saw blue in the darkness and somehow, she believed him. She eased slightly, but he continued to talk. "Oh, I'll have you, but you'll be begging me to fuck you senseless."

Just the thought caused a burning sensation between her legs. Cassandra didn't admit it, but she felt an odd attraction to him. He stood close, causing her to flush and she inched further onto the mattress. "What do you want with me?"

The captor leaned close and yelled, "I want you to shut your fucking mouth."

Chapter 2

ANTHONY LEANED AGAINST the table as he sat and watched Cassandra sleep. Her body was curled up and she shivered in the corner. A part of him felt sorry for her, she had no idea what was going on. One minute she was safe inside her therapist's office, then the next he had shoved her into the trunk of his car. Anthony thought about the day's event.

As Cassandra walked through the parking garage attached to the doctor's office, he walked up behind her, placed his hand over her mouth, and jabbed a needle into her arm. Anthony already rigged the security camera but knew he needed to get her into his trunk, gag and tie her, as fast as he could. He jumped behind the wheel and slowly made his way out of the garage, so not to draw attention to himself. Through the rearview mirror he noticed his accomplice starting Cassandra's car to remove it from the site.

She stirred in her sleep and Anthony focused on her body. It had been years since he'd seen a woman, a desirable woman at least. Hundreds of impure thoughts ran through his mind as his jeans tightened around his crotch. Cassandra had the look he expected a wealthy girl to have—long wavy hair, perfectly aligned teeth, a nice set of breasts, and long toned legs. Anthony longed to undress her, rip her bra and panties off, and have his way with her, but shook his head instead.

Someone of importance had hired him, a man he'd never seen in person. The mission was too important for him to fuck up. He had to stay alert and be ready for anything. Sex was out of the question, though her begging him not to touch her turned him on more than he could admit.

A flip phone on the table vibrated. Cassandra heard it and turned toward him. Her eyes opened as Anthony answered. He covered his mouth and spoke low in the hope she couldn't hear what he had to say. "Yes," Anthony spoke.

"Where is she?" The firm voice on the other end quizzed.

Anthony looked at the girl and lowered his head. "We're exactly where you told me to be."

"No," the boss screamed. "*Where* is she?"

Anthony squirmed in his chair. "She's been sleeping, and her cell phone is locked."

"Holy fuck, kid," the man on the other end of the line burst. "Wake her up and do whatever you have to do to get the phone unlocked. We don't have much time."

He sighed and answered. "Fine. Don't worry, I won't let anything happen to her." Without saying goodbye, Anthony shut the phone and ended the call. Cassandra sat up on the bed and stared at him. He reached inside a drawer and pulled out her phone, then raced over to her side. "Unlock this," he ordered.

"No," Cassandra cried, then hid her face between her knees. Anthony pulled his gun out from the back of his jeans and pressed it against her head.

"Look at me," he barked. Her tear streaked face turned toward him but said nothing. "I said, unlock it."

Cassandra reached over and took the phone in her hands. Her fingers trembled as she keyed in her passcode. She tried to hit the call button, but Anthony grabbed the device and lowered the gun. He sat beside her as he explored her settings and hacked the GPS.

"What are you doing," she stuttered. Anthony looked at Cassandra and smiled.

"I'm not doing anything," he grinned. "You are." He allowed her to watch as he opened her social media app. He then typed, "*Much needed time on the beach*," and hit the send button.

Cassandra's eyes widened as she noticed the location pop up. "No," she shouted.

"What's the matter, you don't like Greece?" Anthony knew he got under her skin and he wanted to laugh.

She choked on her words as she said, "My friends won't look for me if they think I'm on vacation."

The laughter escaped his lungs. "What friends?" he teased.

"I have friends." Cassandra looked down and paused. "In Europe."

Anthony waved the phone in front of her face and continued his torment. "Oh, in Europe," he mocked. "Must have been rough, traveling across the world."

Cassandra straightened herself out and let out a puff of air. "That's none of your business."

Anthony smiled. "Yeah, well I don't think your friends will come to the States to look for you, anyway."

"My therapist knows I'm not planning a trip to Greece."

"Oh yeah, Allen Jenson, the great doctor himself," he laughed. Anthony flipped through her friends list and clicked on the doctor's profile. "Why is your therapist on your social media to begin with? Isn't that a bit strange?"

Cassandra tried again to take the phone, but his hands were too quick. "He's my friend, too."

Anthony shook his head and walked back to the table. She watched his every move, but he didn't care. He turned the passcode off, reset her settings, and then placed the phone in the drawer it came from.

Chapter 3

CASSANDRA SLEPT ON and off throughout the night. The temperature dropped and left her fidgeting to keep warm. If it weren't for whatever poison he put into her body, she wouldn't have slept at all.

She laid in the corner thinking about how her abduction reminded her of her mother's death. Cassandra was young, a mere eight years old, but she remembered it still. Someone was there, she told herself. It was because of those beliefs that her father took her to see a psychologist. In time, along with the help of medication, they convinced her the blue-eyed man she imagined didn't exist.

That doctor, Allen Jenson, continued to council her and became her therapist. Cassandra shook her head when she remembered the stranger asking her why she connected with the therapist on social media. They were friends, she reminded herself, and he would report her missing. Dr. Allen Jenson escorted her to Europe to continue her treatments, claiming it was important for her mental health, and they became friends while abroad. She knew he would look for her.

She turned and noticed the man staring at her. *He doesn't exist*, she heard the voice in her head say. Cassandra wondered why her captor reminded her of the man medication helped her to forget. His eyes, she thought. Cassandra obsessed with blue eyes. She didn't date much, Dr. Jenson said it wouldn't be a good idea, but she'd always been attracted to men with eyes of blue. It was all because of the man who saved her, she thought.

Looking back, Cassandra understood why Allen advised her against relationships. Although he was twice her age, he wanted Cassandra for himself. She liked him, but not in that manner. He once told her, "*I don't see what you like in those colored eyes.*" Cassandra sneered, knowing he said that because his eyes were brown.

She sat up and pulled her knees to her chest. Cassandra had a morning routine which involved taking her medication before she even got out of bed. The stranger continued to watch her. "I need my medication," she told him, assuming he had it.

He shrugged and leaned back in the chair. "No, you don't."

Her mouth gaped at his reply, he didn't know who she was or what she needed. Then it occurred to her that she didn't know who he was, not that it mattered much. "What's your name?" she quizzed.

"What do you care?" He snorted in return.

Cassandra thought about it. "I don't," she replied. "But, since you have me locked up here with nobody else to talk to except you, what harm is it to call you by your name?"

He hesitated but answered, "It's Anthony."

"You mean like Tony," she asked.

Anthony picked up the gun and twirled it around. "You call me Tony and you'll wish you died." Cassandra gulped hard. "They called my no-good father, Tony. Don't make that mistake."

She nodded and sat on the edge of the bed. "Anthony, can I please have my pills?" Cassandra hoped that being polite to him would help her.

"No."

"I need them," she muttered. "They help me, they keep me balanced."

Anthony stood and leaned against the wall that faced her, placed his fist in his front pocket and stared at her. "You don't need shit. Those pills do nothing for you," he told her.

Cassandra worried. If he didn't plan on medicating her, what did he plan? She feared the worst and assumed he wanted to kill her. "Don't you have my purse?" Cassandra asked. "Can't you at least give me my birth control?" She knew didn't have any contraceptives, but if her purse was in the room, she'd be able to sneak her medication when he didn't look.

He chuckled at the thought. "You don't take the pill. You get the shots, and you're not due for another two-and-a-half months."

Cassandra couldn't believe her ears. "How do you know?"

"I know a lot of things, Cassandra Frame." He grinned as she studied his face, but she said nothing for a while. Anthony stood still, telling her he wouldn't back down. She wiggled and held her breath. "Now what's wrong with you?"

"I haven't gone to the bathroom since I've been here," she told him. "I can't hold it much longer," Cassandra admitted.

Anthony walked over to the table and opened the same drawer that held her cell phone to pull out a set of keys. He went to the door and unlocked all the locks. "Well." He turned to her. "Do you have to go or not?"

Cassandra jumped up and followed him out the door and stood in a long dark hallway. Anthony allowed her to walk in front of him. Cassandra thought of making a run for it, but noticed he carried the gun with him. Her feet were bare, and debris covered the floor. She continued walking in the direction he pointed to.

Anthony stopped her at a door. "I'll be right out here," he instructed her.

Cassandra nodded her head and turned the knob. Inside the bathroom was dirtier than the room he held her in. Like the other room, the bathroom had a small basement sized window that let in the sunlight from outdoors. Cassandra almost wished it were still dark.

Cobwebs hung in every corner, and under the sink along the rusted pipes. She neared the toilet and almost vomited. An inch or more of dirt covered the seat, and a stench of death rose from inside. Cassandra cried at the thought of sitting. Her bladder pained her, and she knew she either had to sit on the toilet or let the pee run down her pants.

Cassandra removed her jeans and used them as a barrier between herself and the toilet. It felt good to relieve herself, but she realized there wasn't anything to wipe with. Tears fell down her cheeks as she tried to figure out what to do. Even if there were toilet paper, she told herself, it would have been worthless. She prayed she'd see a clean bathroom before she died.

"You can't flush," Anthony yelled from the other side of the door. "The water is off."

Just great, she complained to herself. Thinking like a man, she wiggled on the seat and tried to get as much of the moisture off as she could. When she stood up to replace her jeans, she could feel the rest of the urine run down her inner thighs. She couldn't end like this, she thought.

Cassandra looked up at the window. She knew her body wouldn't fit through it but hoped she could at least get someone's attention and call for help. Cassandra finished zipping her jeans and knew Anthony could hear her move around. She had to act fast! So, she stood up on an empty trash can, reached for the glass, and pushed. Her footing slipped from the can and she stumbled back to the floor and screamed.

The door burst open and Anthony pulled her out by the arm. "What the fuck are you doing?"

"I tried to wash my hands," Cassandra lied to protect herself. "But a spider came out of the faucet and scared me."

"If there's no water for the toilet, how did you think you could wash your hands?" Anthony yanked her arm and forced her back into the room.

She turned to face him once they were back inside. He re-locked the door and headed back to his chair. Cassandra eyed the locks and wondered if she could figure out which key he used on each of them.

Anthony must have read her mind. Before he sat down, he placed the keys in his front pocket. "If you want them," he teased. "You're gonna have to get them."

Cassandra's face flushed when she looked at the bulge in his pants. Anthony smiled, and she knew she kept her eyes there much longer than she should have. She looked down and raced to the mattress. Cassandra crawled across it and faced the wall.

She didn't want him to see her blush. Her breasts ached, and she knew it was because of him. He had kidnapped her, she reminded herself, and she wondered why her body heated when her mind raced with thoughts of him. Now, more than ever, she needed her medication to keep her from growing insane.

Chapter 4

ANTHONY PACED BACK and forth. The flip phone hadn't sounded, and he grew impatient. Cassandra watched his every move, but he ignored her pleading stares. He didn't like being locked inside the basement any more than she did.

"This place is such a dump," he complained as he kicked the wall and watched the concrete crumble to the floor.

"Then why are we here?" Cassandra asked. She brushed her fingers through her chestnut colored hair and waited for him to reply.

Anthony plopped down on the chair. "It's only for a few days." He looked at her and noticed the way she studied everything he did and said. He realized boredom was getting the better of him and he didn't want to appear to weaken. "Why don't you roll over, go to sleep, and shut up?"

Her stomach growled, and Anthony's agreed. "I'm hungry," she told him.

He reached under the table and pulled out a bag. There wasn't much, and he wasn't sure if it would last. Anthony pulled out a box of crackers and handed her a sleeve while he kept one for himself. He gave her a bottle of water but said, "Don't drink this too fast. We don't have much."

"You didn't bring food and water?" Cassandra rolled her eyes and continued to open her crackers.

"I couldn't exactly carry a ton of groceries and you," he replied. Cassandra dropped her food and bawled. Her tears softened him a little. "Look," he said to comfort her. "I'm not going to hurt you."

She wiped her eyes and looked at him. "Then why are you holding me here?"

Anthony swallowed the food in his mouth an answered. "Let's just say I'm making good on a promise I made a long time ago."

Cassandra didn't know what to think of his comment and he didn't feel like elaborating. She finished the crackers he gave her and rolled over and faced the wall. There was nothing for either one of them to do. She napped on and off for the rest of the day while he continued pacing the floor waiting for the phone to ring.

ANTHONY'S EYES GREW heavy. The sun had gone down outside a few hours before. He hadn't had a good night's sleep in a couple of days and seeing Cassandra sleep on the mattress stirred a little jealousy within him. He watched her as her breathing slowed, and he knew she was out.

He quietly walked over to the mattress and looked down at her. Her eyes didn't open, and Anthony thought that was a good sign. He watched her sleep for a moment. Her soft brown hair enveloped her face. Anthony wanted to bend over and move it away from her eyes but resisted. Touching Cassandra would be a bad idea, he thought.

Moving toward the bottom of the mattress, he slid across to the other side of Cassandra. A pillow would be nice, he thought, a hotel would have been nice too. The boss thought the basement was best until the coast cleared. "He's an idiot," Anthony mumbled to himself.

Cassandra shivered and so did he. The temperature of the basement dropped again. Anthony moved closer to Cassandra and her scent alarmed him. His nose inched closer to her brown locks and took in the Japanese cherry blossom that still lingered. After two long days in a dingy basement, he thought she'd lose the scent.

It wasn't just his nose that moved close to her. Anthony's entire body nestled against Cassandra's. "Shit. This isn't good," he complained again. He knew if she felt his erection press into her, she'd freak out.

He shut his eyes and tried not to think about her soft skin next to him. He promised the boss he wouldn't touch her. It was a job, nothing else, he reminded himself. Part of Anthony hoped she would turn to him and make a move on him, then when the boss found out, he would be innocent.

Finally, sleep found him.

In the morning, when the sun shone through the window, Anthony found his arm stretched over her midsection. He carefully moved it but woke Cassandra. She jumped the instant she realized he had been holding her. "Were you spooning me?"

Anthony stood and put his serious face back on. "I was not spooning you. It was fucking cold in here and if you haven't noticed, there aren't any blankets. Haven't you ever heard of body heat to keep us warm?"

Cassandra shook her head at him and he knew he sounded stupid. Anthony returned to the table. He opened the flip phone but there weren't any missed calls. He flopped in the chair and hoped the boss would call soon.

Chapter 5

CASSANDRA SAT ON THE mattress and followed Anthony with her eyes. He seemed frustrated and she wondered why. She recalled him complaining about their location, heard him on the phone with someone else, and thought he wasn't the one in charge.

"Are you doing this for someone else?" She couldn't believe how brave she acted but needed to know who was out to hurt her.

"Shut up," he snapped again. Cassandra figured out those were his go-to words when he didn't have an answer for her.

She slid closer to the edge of the bed but didn't get off in fear of making him angry. "If you let me go, I swear I won't say a thing." Anthony turned and faced her, and she thought she saw the wheels in his head spin. "Please Anthony," she continued to plead. "You know it's the right thing to do."

Anthony rushed across the room and pushed her back onto the mattress. "I said, shut the fuck up."

Cassandra crawled to the other side and covered her face. She didn't understand her raging emotions. He'd been mean to her, yet Cassandra longed to feel his hands on her again. She wondered what would have happened if she didn't freak out when she woke with him wrapped around her?

She imagined him trailing his hand up her abdomen, resting beneath her swollen breasts before moving up to pinch her nipple between his fingers. Cassandra could feel her panties moisten at the thought. She rolled over and looked at him, slouched in his chair. An image of her straddling him and running her fingers through his hair burned in the back of her eyes, and she couldn't help but grin.

"What the hell are you smiling for?" His harsh words freed Cassandra of her thoughts.

She realized it had been a couple of days without her medication and assumed it caused her hormones to act up. "I will go crazy without my medication. Can I have it?"

Anthony snickered but didn't answer. She fussed on the bed and stood to walk toward him. One way or the other, Cassandra wanted an answer. "You're better off without them," he finally replied.

"No, I'm not." She choked on her words. She couldn't figure out why he'd keep her from something she needed. Cassandra sat back down and cried.

"Go ahead," he instructed. "Cry it out, get it out of your system. Soon you'll realize I'm right about them."

Cassandra didn't have time to argue with him. The flip phone vibrated, and he jumped to answer it. His thumbs maneuvered around the keypad and she knew he received a text. Saying nothing to her, he shoved the phone in his pocket and unlocked the door.

By the time she realized he was leaving, it was too late. Cassandra jumped up and tried to get out the opened door, but Anthony slammed it shut and locked it from the other side. She heard his footsteps walking down the hall and she wondered how long he'd leave her there alone.

Maybe that was his plan, she wondered— to leave her there to rot and die. Cassandra looked to the broken window and grabbed his chair. She placed the chair up against the wall and then climbed on top. Someone had to be nearby who could hear her cries for help. Just as she was about to press on the glass, a leg on the chair snapped and Cassandra came crashing down on her ass. Her arm also felt the blunt of the fall and got scraped. It hurt when she tried to move it.

She cried again in defeat. Cassandra knew she couldn't let a sore arm keep her from trying to get help. She attempted to stand again, but the sound of the door opening stopped her.

"What the fuck?" Anthony screamed and raced to her. "I can't leave you for a freaking minute, can I?" He reached down and yanked her off the floor. His fingers wrapped around her sore arm and she winced in pain.

"I'm sorry," she told him. Cassandra knew better than to make an excuse. It didn't matter anyway, she thought, because it had been obvious what she tried to do.

Anthony ignored her, locked the door, and then punched the wall in anger. Cassandra froze where he left her, too scared to move. His face turned crimson, and she knew he was about to blow. Just then, Anthony's expression changed, and she could see his ear turning toward the ceiling.

She heard it too, a footstep. Before she could mutter a sound, Anthony flew across the room and covered her mouth. Cassandra tried to squirm herself free. Her attempt to open the window failed, but perhaps her attempt to get help didn't. Someone was above them, and she had to let them know.

Anthony held her tight and pulled her over to the mattress. He dove onto it with her in his arms. His grip on her mouth was so tight it caused his fingers to dig deep into her cheeks. She wanted more than ever to scream, but she couldn't.

Cassandra wiggled beneath him, and he wrapped his leg over her body to try and hold her still. When he realized she could still move, he completely enveloped her and put all his body weight onto her.

Trapped beneath him, Cassandra felt her tears run down into her ears. Dust sprinkled down from the ceiling as footsteps shook the floor boards above them. Part of her was scared to death, the other part was relieved there was a search for her. She might not die after all, she told herself.

Sweat from Anthony's brow dripped down on her face. At first it grossed her out. But, by the second drop her hormones had changed again. He was hot, sweaty, and on top of her. Anthony was rough, she was gentle, but the two of them would have burning sex if the opportunity arose.

A few minutes later, they heard the footsteps fade and a vehicle start outside the building. "Thought for sure I heard something," they heard a man's voice state. "Nothing inside though."

Cassandra looked to Anthony and for the first time since the footsteps started, she didn't want to scream. He eased up on his grip but remained on top of her. She knew if she'd ever have the chance to make a move, it couldn't wait. She reached up and cupped the back of his head with her hand, then raised her head until her mouth reached his.

Their lips touched, soft at first, but harder as the seconds ticked away. He pressed into her and bit her lip. She knew he'd been just as hungry for her as she'd been for him. Cassandra opened her mouth and Anthony slid his tongue inside. Lust filled her as he explored the depths of her mouth.

As Cassandra slid her other hand under his shirt and touched his bare skin, he jerked himself away. "What are you doing?" he screamed. Anthony jumped off the mattress and left her lying there, rejected.

She watched him tuck the gun into the back of his jeans and then unlocked the door one more time. Cassandra didn't move. All she could think about was the way he made her feel unwanted. This time she didn't cry, she felt too many emotions to know what to do. So, she stared at the ceiling and thought about what she'd done wrong.

Chapter 6

THE MORNING AIR HIT Anthony in the face as he stepped outside to check the perimeter and make sure the coast was clear. He knew whoever searched the building was looking for him. Cassandra wanted to scream for help, but he knew they weren't there to look for her. He was the one the state wanted.

Sweeping the property for any signs of law enforcement was just an excuse for Anthony. He needed a moment away from her to think about what happened. As much as he wanted her to, Anthony never expected Cassandra to kiss him, not to mention a kiss that burned so much desire between them.

He shook his head and told himself it didn't happen. The boss demanded Anthony to be polite to her, and to keep her safe. He would do that, but he couldn't let Cassandra know. She needed to believe everything that happened or else all hell would break loose.

There was no sign of anyone on the property. Anthony slid along the building and kept silent. He almost let out a sigh of relief but heard someone around the corner. He slouched down behind the unkept bushes.

"I could have sworn I heard something, a crash inside," someone called out.

Anthony detected at least two people remaining nearby. He held his breath and prayed they wouldn't re-enter the building. He couldn't get to Cassandra fast enough and she would scream if she thought there was hope.

"We checked," someone with a voice of authority replied. "Probably just an animal that got inside and knocked something over. We're wasting time, let's go."

Car doors slammed, and tires squealed, telling Anthony they had left. He remained behind the bushes in case it was a trick. A few minutes went by before he crawled to the edge of the building and took a peek, and found the coast clear.

Cassandra collapsed on the bed when Anthony walked in. She almost hyperventilated from crying. It would have been easy for him to comfort her, but he kept his distance. Five minutes of pleasure wasn't worth all the hell he'd catch if he touched her. Anthony knew he wouldn't be able to just embrace her, not after knowing how she affected him. She needed to know who was in charge, and that was him.

"Here," he griped as he tossed a cold sandwich her way. "If you didn't act like a nutcase, you could have eaten this when it was hot."

Cassandra caught the egg and sausage sandwich and unwrapped it. Her mouth was full when she said, "Where did you get this?"

Anthony recalled the text he received stating someone would drop off the food and a few supplies. He wondered if the searchers saw the accomplice's car and followed it? He made a mental note to tell the boss his goons needed to be more careful. "The box," Anthony answered as he looked down. "Duh."

Cassandra smirked. He knew what she really meant, but he wouldn't tell her. The less she knew, the better.

"Thank you."

Antony felt his cock harden when she spoke. He didn't want her to be sweet to him. His life depended on the operation and didn't want his desires for her to interfere. He reached into the box and pulled out a lukewarm cup. As Antony handed it to her, she looked shocked. She took it and gulped it down. Anthony felt bad. There should have been more food and drinks with them. The boss wanted her taken care of, but did a lousy job supplying them with the things they needed.

"This is perfect," she said. "Not hot, but I guess that's my fault, too." Cassandra smiled and turned her head away. "How did you know what I like to drink?"

"I didn't. *He* did. *He* knows everything about you."

"*He*?" She sat up straight when he mentioned someone else.

Anthony knew he shouldn't have, but something inside of him didn't want her to hate him. He fired his gun on the concrete ground to let her know he was through with the conversation, and was glad the gun was equipped with a silencer. The bullet landed nowhere near her, but it scared the shit out of Cassandra. "Didn't I already tell you to stop asking questions?" She finished her breakfast with more tears racing down her cheeks.

ANTHONY WAS AS BORED as Cassandra. He didn't like being caged up and wouldn't have been there if he did. Like the days before, she slept on and off throughout the day. The thought of talking to her for something to do had crossed his mind. The thought of getting to know her scared him.

A stack of boxes along the wall grabbed his attention. Anthony's curiosity got the better of him and he snooped. Old ledger papers, from when the shit hole building was an actual business, filled most of the boxes. He tossed them aside and continued to open boxes.

Cassandra heard the noise and woke up. She watched him but said nothing. Anthony thought she finally learned to keep her mouth shut. The bottom of a box gave out and she giggled. It made her cute, but Anthony ignored her. His muscles bulged while moving the box, but Anthony set it on the table to get a better look inside. "Jackpot," he shouted.

He reached in and pulled out stacks of books. They looked girly to Anthony, and he wondered who would have them in an office. He picked one up and tossed it onto the mattress. Cassandra leaned forward and picked it up.

"Wow," she sounded happy for the first time. "This is one of my favorites."

Anthony wasn't surprised. She looked like a bookworm to him. He stood there and watched her expression. He realized she didn't look like a nerdy bookworm, but someone with a good education. "What's it about?" he asked.

Cassandra told him, but he only pretended to listen. "My father didn't like me reading this when I was younger. I had a copy with me at boarding school until someone ratted me out."

Anthony paused his search through the boxes and looked at her. "He sent you away to school? Is that why you lived in Europe?"

Cassandra looked down as if shamed by her father's actions. "Yes. He said it was because I didn't have a mother to watch over me, and he worked a lot."

Anthony knew she didn't believe the lie any more than he did. Cassandra read, and he dug deeper into the boxes. They were filled with junk, but it gave him something to do. Cassandra screamed. Anthony glanced up and found her tossing the book onto the floor. A spider ran out from beneath it. He laughed at her and continued snooping.

After moving the boxes, Anthony found a tarp that covered more items. He assumed there were more boxes but was wrong. He found a safe, an old refrigerator, and a television. Bingo, he thought.

He picked up the TV and walked it to an outlet near the bed. Cassandra looked bewildered. "If this works," he said, "we'll have something to do."

The television turned on but without cable, it didn't pick up any channels. Anthony left it on and rechecked the unopened boxes for an antenna. Cassandra stared at the snowy screen and covered her ears. He didn't mind when she stood up and lowered the volume. A few minutes later, Anthony found an old-fashioned rabbit ear antenna and hoped it would work.

Cassandra smiled when a picture appeared. It wasn't the greatest reception, but it worked. Anthony changed the channel to search for something better but couldn't find another. He put it back on the only channel it received but frowned when he realized it aired a daytime soap opera.

She watched the show, but Anthony could tell she wasn't into it. Cassandra picked the book up again but shook it over the side of the mattress before reading it. Anthony thought about turning the TV off. They weren't watching it and he thought it could be a risk if someone walked by the building. An urgent news report interrupted the show and changed his thoughts.

"Police are still on the lookout for 32-year-old, Anthony Flint, who escaped from the state penitentiary early on Tuesday morning." Cassandra snapped her head upright and her jaw dropped. Anthony's mug shot appeared on the screen. *"The suspect is reported to be armed and dangerous. He was last spotted-"*

He ran to the other side of the room and pulled the plug. His foot came up and kicked the TV until it fell over, shattering the screen. Cassandra jumped up and backed herself into the corner.

He didn't mean to scare her, although, he was sure the newscast scared her more. The boss would kill him if he found out. "You don't need to see that," he said to her.

She sat on the bed, pulled her knees into her chest and shivered. "What did you do?"

"I broke the television." He played dumb to avoid the question.

"I meant, why were you in prison." She rocked back and forth but didn't take her eyes off him. He wanted her to trust him, but the truth would alarm her.

"Murder." Was all he could say.

Cassandra curled up into a ball and squeezed her eyes shut.

Chapter 7

"THERE WAS NOBODY THERE. I didn't see anyone," Cassandra chanted, over and over. She ran her fingers through her hair and held her head as she rocked back and forth. She took her pulse. There wasn't a clock around, but Cassandra knew her heart beat right out of her chest and her anxiety levels rose fast. "There was nobody there. I didn't see anyone."

Anthony had left with a small plastic bag. She heard the door lock behind him but this time she felt relieved to be left alone. He killed someone, and she feared she would be next.

Her face flushed in the hot basement. "There was nobody there. I didn't see anyone," she continued to convince herself.

"What the fuck are you mumbling over there?" Anthony barged into the room and questioned her.

He stood by the door and looked up. He had bleached his hair, and she wondered how he did it without running water. Cassandra didn't notice the white washed-out marks on the shirt until he pulled it off his body.

She couldn't help but stare at the ripples in his abdomen and the trail of hair leading down into his low-cut jeans. The sight of his half naked, toned body produced moisture in her panties. He's a killer, Cassandra cursed herself. She wished she could control her hormones and eased when he put on another T-shirt.

"I asked you a question," he howled.

She shook her head. Cassandra thought it was none of his business and didn't want to tell him. Anthony dragged his chair toward her and straddled it. He waited for an answer, but she wouldn't give him one. Cassandra's body trembled, and she knew what would still her. Finally, she replied to him, "If I had my pills, I would be calmer."

"Fuck, no." Anthony answered. She snapped her head up and listened to him. "I'll tell you why you can't have them, if you tell me what you've been mumbling."

"There was nobody there. I didn't see anyone," Cassandra repeated, loud enough for him to hear.

Anthony leaned toward her and grinned. "That's why you can't have those pills."

Cassandra was confused and protested. "What?" she squeaked.

"I was there, Cassandra." Anthony spoke to her with a straight face and she realized he knew what she meant by her words.

"No. No. No. This can't be," she babbled. Everything flashed in front of her eyes; her mother's death, the man with blue eyes, and her entire life of being told he didn't exist. "They told me it was my imagination. There was nobody there."

"They said that to convince you. They pumped you with medication to alter your memory." Anthony leaned closer to her and sent goosebumps down her spine. Cassandra couldn't figure him out.

"Why?" Her sobs blossomed to ugly crying.

"If I saved you, behind the crime scene, that would mean I couldn't have—"

Cassandra jumped to conclusions and interrupted. "Oh my God! You killed my mother." She rolled over to the other side of the mattress and jumped off the bed. Anthony reached for her, tried to calm her, but she swatted his hands away. Sweat poured down her face and droplets fell into her cleavage.

He stepped around the bed, closer to her. "Listen to me," he insisted, but she couldn't even look at him. Anthony gripped her shoulders. His fingers dug into her skin. "Listen," he spoke again, in a softer tone.

His words gave her an idea. Cassandra quickly inhaled and looked toward the window. She stared across the room like a deer caught in headlights. Anthony noticed. He turned his head with a questionable brow. "Someone's here," Cassandra whispered.

She called for help, but Anthony placed his hand over her mouth. Her plan was working, but she needed to carry on making it seem real. She continued to cry for someone beneath his sweaty palm. Anthony's ears perked, listening for a sound. He let go of her and raced toward the door. After his exit, Cassandra heard the lock from the other side and knew he would be back soon.

There wasn't much time, she told herself and ran to the other side of the room. The drawer on the table was locked but the table was frail. She picked up a chunk of broken cinder block and pounded it against the drawer. A piece of wood broke off, and she could pry it a little more. All she needed was room for her hand.

Cassandra felt around. It had only been a minute since Anthony went outside, but it seemed like much more. She pulled out her cell phone and pressed the speed dial. "Pick up, pick up, pick up." She panicked.

"Hello," Cassandra's father answered.

"Daddy, I need help," she breathed out into the phone.

"Cassandra? I thought you were in Greece."

"No. There's a man. He kidnapped me. He killed Mom. I need your—"

Anthony knocked the phone out of her hand. She tried so hard to get help and didn't hear him re-enter the room. Cassandra could hear her father call her name. Anthony threw the phone down and stomped on it and she screamed as loud as she could and backed herself into a corner. Anthony picked the cell off the floor and turned the power off.

"What the fuck did you do?" He screamed at her, louder than he ever had. "Do you realize what you've done."

Cassandra's breathing was quick, and her pulse raced. "I need my dad," she tried to say, and hoped he understood.

Anthony pressed her body into the wall. His shoulder pinned her already sore arm in place. Cassandra feared he would strangle her, and she squeezed her eyes shut. The next thing she knew, she felt her body being flung to the floor and landed on a broken piece of glass. She grabbed her leg and noticed blood dripping through a rip in her jeans.

"Holy shit, girl," he continued yelling. "You have no idea."

Cassandra stood, she stumbled back to the mattress and flopped down. Her body ached all over as she crawled back to the wall. She looked at Anthony, afraid of what he'd do next, but instead of coming at her to attack again, he sat at the table.

She watched as he pulled his flip phone from his pocket. "We have a problem." As he spoke his eyes focused on her. Cassandra knew that meant trouble for her.

Chapter 8

ANTHONY GRABBED HER cell phone and keys and shoved them in his pocket. She shivered on the bed, watching his every move, but tried to roll away as he reached for her. He wrapped his hand around her wrist and yanked her off the bed. Cassandra resisted as much as she could, but he pulled her across the room and out of the door.

The boss had instructed Anthony to get her out of the area. He wanted to kick himself for leaving her side and thinking he could trust her. It never occurred to him she'd try to use her phone. "Stupid mistake," he mumbled to himself as he led her down the hallway, up the basement stairs, and out a side door of the building.

"You said you wouldn't hurt me," Cassandra pleaded. Anthony looked down at her raw wrists but didn't ease up on his grip.

Anthony ignored her and forced her to walk beside him. With the gun poked at her side Cassandra obeyed. He led her across a field and entered a woodland area. Anthony glanced around as they fled out of sight and hoped nobody saw them. He felt her dig her feet into the ground as soon as they were in the thick of the woods. Anthony looked to her feet and almost felt bad to see her barefoot. He took her shoes off the day he brought her to the basement, assuming she couldn't run without them. "You have nobody to blame for your pain," he snapped at her.

Cassandra cried as he held her tighter and forced her through the harsh brush. He knew the escape car was nearby, parked it there himself after taking her unconscious body to the basement. He needed to make sure he had easy access to it, but it had to stay where anyone searching for her, or him, wouldn't see. As soon as they reached it, he barked. "Get inside and move over."

Anthony cocked the gun, telling her not to get any ideas about trying to get out the passenger side. Minutes later, the car made its way out to the road and he drove in the opposite direction to the building.

THEY DROVE AROUND FOR more than an hour. The boss told Anthony he would call back with a plan and Anthony looked at the flip phone he placed in the console and hoped it would ring. He didn't understand what took so long. The boss called the shots long before he abducted Cassandra, and Anthony didn't understand why a backup hideaway wasn't thought of before.

He looked down at the gas gauge and slapped his hand against the steering wheel. "Fuck," he said, as he noticed they were down to a quarter of a tank. He didn't know how much longer he could drive around.

"We wouldn't be driving around without a plan if you stayed in prison where you belong," Cassandra snapped.

Anthony couldn't believe he liked her. She turned into a bitch the minute she assumed he killed her mother. "We wouldn't be driving around if you stayed on the bed where you belonged and kept your hands off that God damned phone of yours."

"You're going to get caught, and my father and I will make sure you get put back behind bars," she spit back.

Anthony positioned himself to backhand her but flashing red and blue lights behind him distracted him from his thoughts. "Shit," he murmured. He pulled the car over and shoved his gun between the seats. "You say a word, and he's dead," he said tilting his head toward the approaching officer.

Cassandra shut her eyes and turned her head. Anthony knew she wanted no one to die because of her. He glanced at her then opened the window and turned toward the police officer.

"License and registration," the officer said.

Anthony slowly raised his hands. "They're both in the glove box," he told the officer. The cop nodded as he retrieved the fake papers. He handed them to the officer and smiled at Cassandra. "Is there a problem, Sir?"

"You were swerving. Have you been drinking?"

Anthony felt a flood of relief when he realized the officer wasn't suspicious. "No, Sir," he answered. "My girlfriend fell earlier, and I must have swerved when I looked over to check to see how she's feeling."

Cassandra turned to face the officer. She looked like she'd been in a worse accident than just taking a fall, but the officer didn't appear to think otherwise. "Is this true, Ma'am?"

She nodded her head before speaking. "Yes sir. I missed a step and tumbled down the basement stairs."

Anthony couldn't believe she went with it and the officer bought it. "You should get that looked at," the cop said, as he handed the papers back to Anthony.

"No insurance," Anthony stated.

The officer nodded again. He glanced down at the fake ID and registration in Anthony's hand. "Michael Smith, common name," he snorted.

"Well as they say, I can't choose my parents." Anthony regretted the words as soon as they came out of his mouth. The last thing he needed was to draw attention to himself.

"You look familiar," the officer said. "Take your shades off, son."

Anthony heard Cassandra take a deep breath, like all her troubles were about to go away. He didn't want to stir the pot, so he listened to what the man said. He reached up to take the sunglasses off and turned to face the cop. Anthony looked at him and said, "Could be because all of us Smiths are related to each other."

The officer grinned and tapped the car. "Good point. Drive carefully."

Anthony looked over at Cassandra as the officer walked back to his squad car. He waited until the officer pulled out into the street and drove away before he started to laugh. "Thank God for colored contact lenses," he burst out. Cassandra huffed in disgust and slouched down in the seat. Anthony regained his bearings, figured out where they were, and then continued to drive to a safe spot.

Chapter 9

CASSANDRA STARED OUT the window as Anthony drove in silence. To her, his silence tormented her more than she would admit. She turned to ask him when he put contact lenses in, but the words wouldn't come out of her mouth. She returned to the window and thought about it. Cassandra was distracted by his abdomen when he changed his shirt and didn't notice any other changes about him. The news report, knowing people were searching for him, must have been what urged him to change his appearance. Cassandra sighed a breath of relief, with the change in his eye color maybe she could focus on her safety.

He turned off the highway and descended on a parklike hill. Cassandra stiffened in her seat as she noticed they were out in the middle of nowhere, no houses or businesses nearby. Thoughts of him taking her somewhere private to kill her, crossed her mind. "Where are we going?" She found the courage to ask.

"If we keep driving around we'll run out of gas. There's a lake down here that's not used as much as it used to be. I think we'll be out of sight for a while until my phone rings." He didn't tell her who would call, but Cassandra knew he referred to 'the boss' he spoke of several times before.

Several minutes later he parked the car. Her hand had been laying on the door knob although she hadn't thought of opening it. Anthony reached for the gun, and Cassandra gulped as she removed her hand and placed it on her lap. He continued pointing at her while he reached under the seat. When he sat up, she noticed the roll of rope in his hand. "Please don't," she begged.

"I can't trust you," he replied as he shook his head.

Cassandra winced as he tightened the rope around her wrist, swearing it felt tighter than the last time. She cried out as he double knotted her hands together. "You're hurting me," she whined to deaf ears.

Anthony stepped out of the car and stretched. Cassandra watched as he walked in front of the car and onto her side. "I didn't say you couldn't get any fresh air," he told her as he opened her door. "I just don't want you trying to pull a fast one."

With his help, Cassandra stepped out of the car. She nodded her head toward the water as if asking if she could go near it. Anthony said nothing but kept his eyes on her. She walked to the shore and placed her sore feet in the water. For a moment, Cassandra felt relieved but knew she wasn't out of danger. She glanced around and began to figure out where they were.

After she returned to the car, Anthony handed her a bottle of warm water. This time, with tied wrists, she maneuvered the bottle better and drank with ease. Anthony gulped his bottle down and moaned, "I have to take a piss."

He walked toward the lake and Cassandra made a run for it. She wasn't far from civilization after all and needed to get away from the murderer. Her legs took long strides as her arms clung to her chest. She heard Anthony swear and knew he would catch her, still she had to at least try.

She didn't get too far away when Anthony's body came crashing down on her. They tumbled to the ground. Pain seared throughout her body as he covered it with his own. She cried out and continued her attempt to get away, but Anthony covered her mouth with his hand and didn't remove it even after she bit down. She saw anger rage through him and longed for his touch. Cassandra crawled backwards, but he pressed his hard body into her. Anthony's knee pressed against the innermost part of her thigh, creating a fire in her jeans.

"Stop," he screamed at her, as she continued to wiggle away from him. Anthony pinched her cheeks together and forced her to look at him. "Damn it, girl. I'm not supposed to tell you this."

Cassandra paused when he spoke. Her curiosity rose. "Tell me what?" she mumbled underneath his hand.

He straddled her body and let go of her mouth. Cassandra knew if she screamed, he wouldn't tell her. She lied still and waited until he spoke.

"I'm not the bad guy, my boss isn't the bad guy, either. Stop running from me."

Anthony's weight eased up and Cassandra pulled herself into a sitting position. He reached for his gun and she knew better than try to run. "If you're not the bad guy, why are you pointing that at me?"

"For your safety," he replied. "More to scare you than anything else." Anthony sat beside her but gripped her arm just in case. "Please stop running from me."

Cassandra didn't know what to think. She couldn't figure out why her mother's killer escaped from prison to kidnap her, but claimed he wasn't the bad guy. "If you're not the bad one, who is?"

"I can't tell you," Anthony answered. Cassandra inched away from him, not believing a word he said. "Look, the boss will have a fit when he finds out I'm telling you this much, but I'm not the one who killed her. They did, and now they want you dead too."

"I don't understand," she told him. "Why were you in prison if you didn't murder my mother?"

Anthony reached over and for the first time, held her hand gently. "They told you, convinced you, I wasn't there that night, but I was, Cassandra. You were right all along. Do you remember? I told you I'd be right back." She shook her head, not knowing what to think. "I'm a little late, but I'm here now, just like promised."

Cassandra bawled her eyes out. Nothing made sense, yet everything made perfect sense. She needed to know what was going on. "If you're telling me the truth, why were you in prison?" She knew she already asked him but felt he didn't give her the correct answer.

"I left you to check on her, hoping she was still alive." Anthony's eyes glistened as he told his side of the story. "As I bent over to check her pulse, the police arrived. I tried to explain, but nobody listened and they arrested me. Your father wanted a quick conviction so his family name wouldn't be dragged through the mud. I couldn't afford a good attorney, and the jury believed them and sent me away for a crime I didn't commit."

Cassandra cried harder and felt herself lean against his shoulder. The memories that surfaced caused more pain than anything physical he could ever do to her. She felt his arm wrap around her as she nestled closer to him. "Oh my God, were you the one who saved me that night?"

"Yes," Anthony answered. "They medicated you and convinced you I didn't exist because if you could testify my location at the time of the shooting, I would have been found innocent and set free." Cassandra hid her face between her legs and sobbed. "We've kidnapped you to hide you from the killers."

Cassandra's head snapped up. He'd been trying to tell her about them since she fled moments before, but she hadn't been paying attention. "Who are they, and why do they want me dead now?"

"They wanted you dead then, too," Anthony told her. "If I didn't show up before the cops did, you would have died the same night as your mother."

The ground was unsteady as Cassandra tried to stand. Anthony stood beside her and pulled out a pocket knife. He cut through the rope but kept his eyes on her. "Thank you," she wept.

Anthony put his arm around her waist to steady her. "If you like life, you'll stop trying to get away from me and let me protect you."

They walked back to the car and sat inside in silence. Cassandra pulled the hair off her face and tried to knot it behind her head to keep it in place. A million things ran through her mind. "Is my father's phone tapped?"

"What?"

"We wouldn't be on the run if I didn't call him," she answered as she figured pieces of the puzzle out. "Can they tell where I am because I called him?"

Anthony leaned over the steering wheel and stared out into the dusky sky. "Something like that," he answered. "I had you post from Greece to give us some time, but since you made a phone call here in the States, they will know you're not there."

Cassandra hung her head. If they found her, and succeeded at killing her, she knew it would be her fault. Her tears dried up as she sat in shock. Anthony swore again as he threw the flip phone down. His entire story could have been a lie, anything to convince her to stay with him, but somehow, she believed him. They waited to find out where to go to keep her safe.

It gave her an idea. "We have a house on the other side of this lake."

Anthony turned his head and gave her a questionable brow. "What do you mean?"

"I realized where we were when I washed up in the lake earlier. That's where I planned to go when I tried to run from you. Can't we wait it out there?"

A smile spread across his face. "How far is it?"

"About fifteen minutes, maybe a little more if we have to stay off the main roads."

Chapter 10

THE BOSS PICKED UP on the second ring, and Cassandra looked at Anthony but remained quiet. He thought the lake house sounded great but couldn't make any moves without informing the boss.

"She knows about them," Anthony said when the man in charge answered.

Cassandra could hear the other man freak out. "What?" he screamed into the phone.

Anthony looked at Cassandra, who had her head lowered in shame. "I had to tell her. She kept trying to run away. What else could I do?"

The boss sighed and didn't reply for a few moments. Finally, he asked, "Is she alright?"

Cassandra heard the other man ask about her and lifted her head. Anthony looked over to her as he replied. "She's scared and to be honest, I don't blame her." There was silence on the line until Anthony continued. "Listen, Cassandra told me about a lake house nearby. I'm running out of gas. Do you think it's safe?"

The boss didn't answer right away. Anthony could almost hear the gears in his head. The boss knew Cassandra's family and knew what house they talked about. "Yes, go there for a night or two, but no longer. Be smart and keep a look-out."

Anthony hung up the phone and nodded at her. Cassandra twist her body toward him as he gripped the steering wheel until his knuckles turned white. A place to stay was great, but they were still in danger and they still needed gas.

"Your purse is in the trunk," he told her. "You have any money for gas?" Cassandra laughed. "Hey, I didn't look inside it. I didn't want to be charged with kidnapping and robbery." Her smile stretched across her face and she held her stomach. Anthony laughed, too until Cassandra started to cry. "Hey, it's ok." He comforted her. "I'm sorry we had to go about it this way, abducting you and treating you like a hostage. It's for your own good."

She wiped her eyes with the back of her hands. "I have credit cards."

"No." Anthony shook his head. "They can be traced."

"But, you said no one would look for me."

"That was before you used your cell phone and let the real killers know you were still in the area. They used their power to wrongfully convict me. They'd use it to track your credit cards down, too."

Cassandra nodded her head in agreement. The sun was going down and dusk settled in. They needed to get to the lake house as soon as they could. He popped the trunk and walked to the rear of the car. For the first time, Cassandra didn't run.

Anthony handed her the purse when he reentered the car. She reached in and pulled out her wallet. As luck would have them, she had a few twenty-dollar bills wadded together. Cassandra gave him a toothy smile. Damn, she's cute, he said to himself.

Anthony backed the car out and headed in the direction they came from, he hoped the darkness would conceal them. He was still a wanted felon in the state's eyes, people still looked for him, and God only knew where the goons that wanted her dead were.

At the gas station he pumped the gas and Cassandra went inside to pay. It was too risky to let anyone see him up close even though he wore a disguise. Anthony kept his eyes out for any danger, but there didn't appear to be any.

Cassandra came out with a small bag. Without asking her what was inside, Anthony hightailed it away from the gas station. She told him where to go and then leaned back in her seat. Cassandra looked more relaxed now that she knew the truth. Somehow, Anthony thought, he went from being her abductor to being her protector.

"They almost didn't serve me." She laughed. "They said, 'No shoes, no service,' but I lied and told them I forgot them at the beach."

"They must have believed you," said and smiled. She reached into the bag and pulled out two bottles of soda. She opened one and handed it to Anthony. "Thank you," he said, and then thought to himself that things should have been that easy from the start.

"I would have bought more," she said as she looked in the bag of snacks, "but I figured we didn't have too much time."

Anthony couldn't help but grin. He never imagined she'd understand the situation. "You did fine," he said, and continued to drive away.

IT WAS DARK BY THE time they got to the lake house. There wasn't a sign of anyone being around for miles. Anthony thought it was a good sign, though it concerned him, too. They got out of the car and Cassandra located the hidden key.

"It's not a good idea to leave the car out in the open," he told her. Cassandra held her finger up to tell him to wait. She opened the main door of the house and turned to walk inside. Anthony grabbed her arm and stopped her. "Not until we know it's safe inside."

He reached for her hand as they entered the house together. Her warmth spread up his arm, giving him chills. They edged their way through the dark entrance and found the inside door to the garage. It opened, and Anthony stepped out. Cassandra remained on his heels.

The garage was dark, but Anthony shined a flashlight around. When he knew for sure there wasn't anyone else there, Anthony gave Cassandra a nod. She pressed a button on the wall and the garage door rose. He ducked down and stepped out to the other side.

Cassandra moved to the steps leading up to the house to get out of the way. Anthony pulled the car inside and parked it next to a sharp looking black BMW. "It's Daddy's," she told him, as he looked it up and down. "He only drives it when we're up here."

Anthony held the flashlight against the window but saw nothing out of the ordinary inside. He glanced over the garage again but saw nothing to cause alarm. After shutting the door, he turned the light off, making it pitch dark inside.

"What are you doing?" Cassandra questioned him.

"Look for blinking lights," he instructed her. They both scanned the room but found nothing. Anthony turned to face her. "We're good. No cameras or bombs."

They entered the house. Anthony walked through with the flashlight in one hand and Cassandra in the other. Cassandra jumped at every shadow they crossed. Though she no longer feared Anthony, she still feared for her life.

"It's better to stay in the dark," he said. "Just in case."

Their eyes adjusted as the moonlight shone off the lake and through the windows. Cassandra let go of his hand and sat down. Anthony joined her.

"Can I shower?"

Anthony wanted to shower with her, his way of keeping her safe, but didn't think she'd find his humor funny. He couldn't allow any mistakes that would get them caught again. "I think we're safe here, but I don't know about having a light shine from inside the house."

"The guest bathroom is down the hall and doesn't have a window," she told him. "Come on, I'll show you."

Cassandra walked him down the hall and was right about the lack of a window. The thought of being cleaned tempted him and he couldn't resist. Anthony looked down at his dirty jeans and wished he could change. He wondered if she had spare clothing there, and what the odds were there were clothes for men. "You have any clothes here, for yourself and for me, I mean for men?"

"Yes." Cassandra walked with him down the hall and entered a bedroom. She took the flashlight from him and shone it on a dresser. Inside, there were shorts and shirts of all sizes. Anthony gave her a puzzled look. "For when we have company and go for a swim."

The shorts weren't fancy, but they were clean. He agreed to let her shower. Cassandra led him up the stairs and into her bedroom. There was a large window and Anthony feared the flashlight would shine for miles. He told her they had to rely on the moonlight again while she located clean clothes. Cassandra understood and led him back downstairs when she finished.

Chapter 11

ONCE THEY REACHED THE bathroom Anthony cautiously checked behind the shower curtain. He knew nobody would be there since his initial walk-through of the house confirmed they were alone. But, he wanted to make sure there wasn't anything of danger lurking in unexpected places. When it checked out, he returned his attention to Cassandra.

"We should clean up those cuts on your arm," he suggested.

Cassandra opened the medicine cabinet and pulled out anything she thought could help her. She quickly inhaled when he placed a swab soaked with peroxide on her tender flesh. The wounds bubbled, and she knew he'd been right about taking care of them. He sealed the area with adhesive bandages.

She couldn't help her rapid heartbeat as Anthony stood face-to-face with her, his hot breath fanned her skin. His hands shook as he tended to her injuries and Cassandra wondered if he wanted her as much as she wanted him. "I think my leg is worse," she whispered.

"Your leg?" he questioned, but then looked down at her jeans as if he remembered throwing her across the basement. "You better take off your pants."

Cassandra's cheeks flushed but the throbbing pain on her shin told her to obey him. She unzipped her jeans and slowly wiggled them off her hips. Cassandra looked at Anthony as her panties came into sight and noticed the smile on his face, but he looked away when she made eye contact. Seconds later, she stood before him in dirty underwear and wished she never mentioned the wound on her leg.

He knelt and held the back of her knee with one hand while the other hand wiped the swab over the injury. Cassandra realized his face neared her crotch, and her body craved his touch. Just a split second before she found the courage to offer herself, Anthony stood and backed away. "That should do," he declared, then walked out of the bathroom.

Anthony sat outside the bathroom as Cassandra showered. She left the door unlocked, just in case he needed to get inside for any reason. The hot water rushed over her aching body. Cassandra leaned against the wall and clenched her fist together. Her ordinary boring life had turned into a crazed nightmare.

Her thoughts turned to her father. Cassandra prayed they weren't after him, too. She wouldn't know what to do if anything happened to him. Life was hard enough without a mother, if she lost her father, too, it would devastate her. Her maternal grandmother had recently passed away, and she was the last of her mother's family.

Her father stood by her side, during her Grandmother's funeral, and held her hand. He hadn't communicated with anyone from her mother's side of the family since she died fifteen years before. It took Cassandra years to realize how hostile they were toward each other, though he never tried to stop her from spending time with her grandmother.

Cassandra turned the water off and stepped out onto the soft carpet. She toweled herself off as fast as she could. The thought of being naked when someone killed her, scared the crap out of her. The sound of the air conditioner kicking on caused Cassandra to wrap the towel around her body and run out of the bathroom.

Anthony stood up when she opened the door. She jumped into his arms. "What happened?" He asked as he lifted her chin.

"Nothing," Cassandra stuttered. Her entire body shook. "I don't want to die."

He pulled her close to him and wiped the moisture from her eyes. "You're not going to die, Cassandra. You weren't supposed to know any of this, but it is helping me protect you."

Anthony's lips were close to Cassandra's. She wanted to kiss him again, but resisted the urge. She pulled back and straightened herself up. Anthony walked into the bathroom, leaving Cassandra alone in the dark hallway. They were in her family vacation home, she told herself, and her tension eased a little. When she heard the water start within the bathroom, she dropped her towel and slipped into the clean clothes. Cassandra sat down and waited for him, like he had for her moments before.

The bathroom door opened, and Anthony stood before Cassandra. He looked ridiculous in the shorts he picked out and she giggled. He reached for her hand and pulled her to her feet.

"I'm hungry," she told him, and assumed he would be hungry too. "There's stuff in the freezer, but I doubt there's anything fresh since we haven't been up here in weeks."

"Anything microwavable?"

Cassandra shrugged her shoulders, and they walked to the kitchen together. Anthony opened the refrigerator; the light almost blinded both. Cassandra searched the cupboards but found nothing appealing. Anthony found frozen pizzas, perfect for the microwave.

Cassandra nuked the food while Anthony closed the curtains in the living room. He stubbed his toe on an end table as he made his way back into the kitchen. She handed him two glasses of soda then removed the hot food from the microwave. "We can eat this in here or in the living room," she told him. Anthony walked back to where he'd just came from and sat on the couch.

As they ate, thoughts of being killed ran through Cassandra's mind. "Is anyone trying to capture these men? Or am I on the run for the rest of my life?"

Anthony swallowed his food and leaned back onto the couch. He slipped his fingers through his wet hair. "The boss is trying to nail the bastards," he informed her. "I can't tell you much more. Just know, you're not going to die or have to hide for the rest of your life."

Cassandra sighed, but her nerves still rattled. She ate half of her pizza but knowing someone was after her caused her appetite to dwindle. She offered the plate to Anthony who took it and guzzled it down.

"Are you really helping me because of a promise you made fifteen years ago?" Cassandra couldn't help but think there was more to it.

Anthony didn't answer right away, and she assumed he ignored her. She stood to take the dishes back to the kitchen, but Anthony reached for her forearm and she sat back down.

"Yes and no," he answered. "I've said this before, this is a job. My boss has big connections and can have me pardoned if I succeed at keeping you safe."

Cassandra realized she was aiding an escaped felon. She done nothing wrong in her life. A week before, if she knew the whereabouts of a con, she'd call the cops. Times changed. She needed this man in so many ways.

She yawned. It had been another hard day, but at least she would have the comfort of her own bed. "I'm tired," Cassandra told him. "I'll be up in my room."

Anthony stood up and walked behind her. "Not alone, you won't be."

"What?"

"Both of our lives depend on me watching you. To play it safe, we're sleeping together."

Cassandra's knees turned into jelly as she stood. The pizza in her stomach turned and threatened to come back up if she didn't control herself. He'd slept beside her in the basement and nothing happened. That was different, she told herself. Anthony was the enemy then, now he was putting his life on the line for her. Cassandra wasn't sure if she could keep her hands to herself.

She turned to face him. Her cheeks burned, and she prayed he couldn't see them. "Alright," she moaned, but it sounded too much like pleasure.

"Don't worry," he grinned. "You'll be in good hands."

Chapter 12

ANTHONY FOUND IT HARD to sleep next to Cassandra's soft body. She had her back turned toward him, her leg bent and lifted over the other one. He glanced down at the round flesh peeking out of her shorts and his dick hardened. Anthony wanted nothing more than to roll her over and pull her into his hardness.

The sun came through the window when he woke. He wasn't sure how long he slept, but he knew she'd slept longer. Cassandra inched closer to him at some point. Her arm stretched and rested on his chest. Anthony watched her, but not for long. He felt himself growing hard, but knew there was no way he could take advantage of the girl.

He knew if he gave into his desires, his focus would shift, and he wouldn't be on high alert for the killers. The boss would see Anthony dead if anything happened to Cassandra. It was best to keep his eyes, and hands, off her.

Anthony slipped out of the bed, but she heard him.

"Good morning," Cassandra whispered.

Fuck, he thought, she was too freaking sexy. He didn't reply, just stood up and walked toward the window. The sun glistened on the lake. Anthony never seen green water sparkle like that. Cassandra stood behind him, a little too close for comfort, and pressed her head against the window.

"You probably take this view for granted," he said.

"Actually," she corrected him. "No, I don't. I love nature and being outdoors. Can we swim?"

Her question threw Anthony off guard. Those goons could've been anywhere. "I can't answer that right now," he told her. She looked down and frowned.

Anthony locked her in the room while he checked the perimeter of the property. Cassandra understood. All the doors and windows to the house were locked, the garage was tight, too. He tucked his gun into his shorts and slinked around the property. There was no sign of trespassers.

He locked the door behind him as he walked back inside. The flip phone vibrated, and he answered. "Yeah, we're good here. Any leads on those bastards?"

"Seems they had a slight problem catching a flight back from Greece," the boss informed. Anthony was sure he pulled a few strings. "We have their locations locked in. You're safe for at least another day or two, maybe less, so always be on alert. Their leader is in the area, but I don't think he has the balls to do the job himself. Too much at risk."

"You think he'll come here?" Anthony gulped as he thought about it. There was always the possibility and, unlike the boss, Anthony didn't trust that their leader wouldn't try to kill Cassandra himself.

The boss paused before answering. "No, he's at a conference. Word has it, he planned it to cover his ass. Alibi."

Anthony sighed. It all made sense, he wouldn't want an association with the murder of Cassandra Frame. "And what about the police?"

"Haven't you seen the television?"

They spared the use of electricity in fear of being seen, but now that daylight arrived, Anthony saw no reason not to turn the television on. He stepped into the living room and picked up the remote. "What channel?" he asked.

"Seven."

"*Authorities tell us that a man fitting the description of Anthony Flint boarded a plane to Mexico late last night. Local police are working with the FBI to attain the man once they locate him. For now, residents can rest easy knowing the convicted killer is not in the area.*"

"No shit," he exclaimed into the phone. "How did you pull that off?"

The boss didn't answer. He never told Anthony the big details, only what he needed to know to keep Cassandra safe. "Always be on the lookout," the boss scolded. "And keep a low profile. I'll contact you as soon as I have any word."

CASSANDRA STARTLED when Anthony unlocked the bedroom door, but smiled when she realized it was him. He couldn't help but smile back. "Breakfast is ready, are you hungry?"

She stepped closer, a wave of sweet perfume invaded his nostrils. Every little thing she did drove Anthony crazy. "You have to ask?" Cassandra's laugh echoed in the room. She brushed her hand against his as she passed.

Anthony led the way to the back deck where the table was set. Cassandra couldn't take her eyes off it. He pulled a chair out for her and then sat opposite. She grabbed the carafe and poured two cups of coffee. Anthony knew she preferred chai, but he couldn't find any. Cassandra didn't seem to mind.

They ate pancakes and bacon, the only meat he could find in the freezer, in the morning sun. Birds were singing in the distance, but Anthony listened to the sound of crickets near the water. "Do you like to fish?" he asked her, but thought it was a stupid question to ask a rich girl.

Cassandra wiggled her nose, just like he expected her to answer. "No, why?"

"Dinner," he told her. He figured since they were out on the lake for a day or two, they might as well take advantage of it. "You eat it, right?"

Cassandra laughed again, this time he joined her. "Yes, but I don't know how to cook it."

They finished breakfast and cleaned up. Cassandra reclined on an Adirondack chair as Anthony snooped around for fishing gear. He found two poles and laid them on the deck. She shook her head and read a book. He stepped off the deck and moved rocks around. After a few minutes, he had collected a handful of worms.

Anthony dangled one in front of Cassandra and she screeched. As he got closer, she covered her face with her hands and tried to move away. "Come on," he teased her. "It's just a worm."

"It's disgusting," she snapped at him, but he laughed.

He reached for her hand and pulled her off the chair. She wanted to read but he couldn't leave her alone. She reluctantly followed him down a path toward the water. Cassandra sat on the ground while he stood. The worm wiggled as Anthony stabbed it with the hook. "You're gonna have to get a little closer," he said to Cassandra.

"Oh, no," she said, and shook her head. Her chestnut hair landed on her shoulder. "I'll watch."

He took her hands and brought her up to her feet. He knew she didn't know what she was missing and, he wanted to be the one who introduced her to new things. Anthony placed the rod in her hand and stood close behind her as he showed her how to hold it. He felt her skin against his as he held her hand in place. She faced him and grinned, like she knew what he thought. Anthony helped her cast the line into the water.

The line flew out. "Great," he told her. "Now keep it there. Stay still."

Anthony tended to his pole. He could barely hook it before she got excited. "Something is happening," she gleamed.

Cassandra's pole arched, and she almost dropped it. Anthony ran and stood behind her. Her hair blew in his nose and blood rushed south again. They stood close as he reached his arms around her to help her control her fishing pole. "Feels like a big one," Anthony said.

"It sure does," she replied.

Chapter 13

ANTHONY FILLETED THE fish as Cassandra gathered towels for their swim. She glanced at him and could have sworn she saw a pout on his face. It wasn't her fault she'd caught more fish than him, she thought. She never thought she'd like to fish but couldn't contain her excitement every time she caught one. He smirked when Cassandra caught her fifth and said they had enough.

The sun beat down on her as she opened a can of soda and watched him clean the fish and was glad he didn't make her help. "Do you want one?" she asked, lifting the can.

"When I'm done," he told her without looking up.

When he was on the last fish, Cassandra walked inside to grab another can. She looked at the landline and thought about her father. He must have wondered where she was, she thought. Cassandra picked up the receiver and placed her finger on the first button. Anthony's hand collapsed on hers and forced her to put the phone down. He growled as he yanked the cord out of the wall.

"I wanted my father to know I'm not hurt."

Anthony grabbed the drink and pushed her onto the deck. "Do you ever think?" He yelled and all of a sudden, Cassandra felt like his captive again. "They have the phone line bugged."

"How do you know?" she couldn't help but ask. Cassandra hadn't seen him that angry since he told her the truth.

He grunted and grabbed the towels she laid on the table. Cassandra followed his quick steps to the dock. He paused half way and his face softened as he looked at her. She tried to keep up. "Cassandra, they're trained assassins. Trust me, they know everything there is about you."

"I'm sorry," she told him. She wanted them to relax again, like they had been doing all morning.

Anthony put the towels and his drink down. Cassandra's mouth watered as he pulled his shirt over his head. She wanted an excuse to touch him as the devil in her came to life. He didn't notice her step closer to him, or see her hands stretch out to push him. Splash! Cassandra didn't think of the consequences beforehand.

Anthony resurfaced, and she buckled over in laughter. "Oh, game on, girl." He laughed as he pulled himself up the ladder. Cassandra realized she was in trouble and ran down the dock. Anthony caught her and lifted her up in the air. She begged him to stop. "Please don't," she panted.

His wet body held her tight and Cassandra wrapped her arms around his neck, assuming he couldn't throw her. "You're nothing but trouble." He chuckled. "And troubled girls need a lesson about cold water."

There was no time to plead her case. He jumped with her in his arms. "Oh. Em. Gee. The water is freezing." Cassandra squealed when she came up for air. His hands let go of her and they swam to the shore. She tried to stand up, but he pulled her back in.

Cassandra shivered in the waist-high water. Anthony splashed her, and she covered her face from his wrath. He wrapped his hands around her hips and lifted her in the air before tossing her back under water.

She came up gasping for air as he laughed. Anthony stood close to her. "You didn't give me a chance to take my shirt off." Cassandra crossed her arms and struggled with the wet T-shirt. Anthony leaned in to help her and her nipples perked up. There was no way she could hide them. Anthony grinned. His warm hands slid across her back and pulled her close to him. Cassandra hoped he'd kiss her. She leaned her head back and stretched her neck, expecting his lips on hers.

"That's what you get for pushing me," Anthony said, as he submerged her in the water.

An hour passed, and they still swam. The sun burned on their skin, causing the water to feel good instead of cold. Cassandra pulled herself up onto the dock and plopped down on the wood. "I need a drink," she said. Anthony followed and sat beside her.

He took her can and swallowed the rest of it. Cassandra attempted to protest, but he leaned back and she fell onto his chest. Her pulse raged as he reached up and pulled her closer. Cassandra studied his face and admired the way the sun sparkled in his blue eyes.

His hand crept up her thigh, his grip hard. He adjusted her until she was on top of him. Cassandra leaned down and his mouth met hers. This time, she knew he wanted her as bad as she wanted him. Cassandra opened for him and Anthony's tongue explored the depths of her.

He flipped her and leaned over her. Cassandra's legs wrapped around his waist as his hand held hers above her head. Her lips trailed to his ear and traced his lobes. She felt him press into her and she breathlessly quivered. He ran his lips over her face and made his way down her neck.

Cassandra shifted below him as he nibbled on her bikini top, bringing the fabric down with his teeth, and exposed her breast. Anthony arched his back then circled her nipple. "Anthony," she cried out with pleasure. He didn't stop, just repeated the same pattern on the other breast.

Cassandra's hands were still above her and she couldn't break free. "Shhh." He breathed into her ear. The hand that wasn't holding hers moved and slid down her torso. Cassandra never felt more alive. He touched every inch of her side, sending chills down her spine.

Anthony rubbed her inner thigh as her legs spread further apart. He rested his forehead on hers and kissed her as he fumbled with her bathing suit bottoms. The strings were easy to untie, leaving Cassandra naked beneath him.

He flicked his thumb against her nub and the sky above them changed from blue to pink and orange, she thought. He stretched a finger along Cassandra's already moist folds and weighed his mouth harder on hers. Cassandra's ass lifted off the dock as Anthony's magical finger slipped deep inside of her.

Cassandra's hands grabbed onto Anthony's shoulders as soon as he released them. He twisted his fingers inside of her and she saw stars in the daytime. Her lips attacked his neck and then kissed him all over his torso. Cassandra felt her foot sliding up his leg, opening further for him.

"Ready for another lesson?" he panted. Sweat dripped off him and melted on her skin. Her body scorched and desired all he offered. She smiled and nodded, words were momentarily foreign to her.

Anthony reached down and held himself. She could feel his knuckles rub against her stomach as he aimed his hard dick in her direction. He teased her for a few minutes. Cassandra took a deep breath and tossed her head. Between the hot sun and his sexuality, she was at a loss. "Oh God, yes," she answered.

He pushed forward and tore into Cassandra. She gasped for air as his fingers gripped her ass harder than before. "Holy shit, Cassandra. Are you a virgin?"

"I was," She answered, her body mixed with agony and pleasure. "There's more than one reason for a girl to be on birth control."

Anthony froze and looked down. She wanted his sex and he needed to know that. She smiled and reached up to kiss him again. He held her tight and pulled her to his chest. "I didn't mean to hurt you. It will feel much better really soon."

"I'm ok," she assured him.

Anthony rocked himself. His hardness inched deeper into her. A whirlwind of emotions raced through Cassandra, causing her body to react to him. He put his hand on her hip and guided her to rock with him. Cassandra raised her bottom again and followed his lead.

The pain lessened a few minutes later. Anthony sucked on her nipple again as she ran her hand up and down his back. He moaned in delight and Cassandra hoped he wouldn't finish. She never wanted the moment to end.

He couldn't control himself and she felt him shake. Anthony thrusted hard, causing Cassandra more pain. His body convulsed as he squeezed her ass. "I'm gonna come," he told her. A hot fire burned inside of her. Cassandra's head hit the dock. She wanted more, much more.

Chapter 14

ANTHONY DIDN'T REGRET a thing after having sex with Cassandra. He knew it wasn't just lust, there was something else about her that captivated him. He'd been locked up for years, and in some strange way, so had she, only she didn't realize it. Anthony had been a prisoner of the state while she'd been a prisoner of her father. Cassandra's father shipped her off to boarding schools across the world, away from her loved ones, and that alone determined Anthony's thoughts on her freedom.

Although they had come from complete different backgrounds, he could tell that she understood him and saw him for who he truly was. Sure, he thought, she'd been difficult, but her soul called to him. Anthony already decided he would claim her when the rocky road ahead of them calmed. He wanted her, in every way, and he knew she'd accept him.

The boss would have a conniption fit when he found out about their affair. Anthony's job was to protect her, to hide her from the men who wanted to kill her, and when the true culprits were caught, he'd get a pardon for his crimes.

As he fried the morning's catch, Cassandra swayed in front of him. Anthony grinned at her flirtatious body language, but cursed himself for being stupid and careless. It wasn't the sex he cursed himself about, but he took her right out on the dock where they could have been targets like sitting ducks.

She set the table and microwaved a bag of frozen vegetables. There wasn't much food in the house, but they weren't starving. As Anthony placed the fish on a serving dish, Cassandra wrapped her arms around him from behind and cupped his groin. "Not now," he complained and pushed her away. Blood rushed to the area, but he needed to be on guard to protect her. Cassandra batted her eyelashes and looked down. She looked hurt and he couldn't handle upsetting her. He reached for her hand and pulled her close to him. "It's not that I don't want you. I just need to be more careful. They're still out there and I won't let anything happen to you."

Cassandra rested her head on his shoulder for a second, then reached up and kissed his cheek. "You once told me I'd be begging you to fuck me senseless, and you were right. I get it though and appreciate it." He squeezed her tight and kissed her forehead. "Just know, I'm not done begging yet." They both laughed, then continued preparing for dinner.

The flip phone vibrated on the counter and Cassandra threw him a concerned look as he leaped forward to answer it. "Yeah," he said.

"You need to leave now," the boss informed him. "Their plane just landed." He huffed, sounding annoyed like someone didn't report to him fast enough. "If that's not bad enough, FBI agents down in Mexico didn't find you on that plane and they now assume you're still in the area."

"Holy shit," Anthony shouted. He turned his back to Cassandra and looked out the glass door as he spoke. "Where should we go?"

"There's an abandoned warehouse," the boss told him and gave him the address and directions. "I think we might need to revert to Plan B. This will all be over soon, and I have men working on the arrangements now."

Anthony knew what Plan B was, but knew it was best not to mention it to Cassandra. She wouldn't understand and now that she tugged on his heartstrings, he wasn't sure he wanted to continue with the plan. He didn't have a choice but to agree. "On it," he choked on the words. "I'll alert you when we get there." Anthony flipped the phone closed and shoved it in his pockets.

"What's happening?" she questioned.

"We don't have much time. Grab something to throw this food into, gather as many things as you can in five minutes—food, toiletries, blankets."

Cassandra dropped to her knees and fumbled through plastic ware in the cupboard. "Are we going back to the basement?"

Anthony ran into the garage to grab her phone and came back seconds later. "No, although I'm not sure of the new place's condition so we'll take as many things as we can, but we have to hurry."

While she went off to gather belongings, Anthony turned her cell phone on and checked her GPS. Everything checked out. He left the phone on and shoved it underneath the couch. Cassandra walked by with two garbage bags full of necessities. "What are you doing?"

"They'll be here soon," he informed her. He could see the bewilderment look on her face and continued. "Don't ask me how I know, instincts I guess. But, when they track your cell phone, they'll think you're here and will waste time searching the property. It'll give us a little time to get away."

Anthony grabbed the bags with one hand, and her with the other. They raced out to the garage and Cassandra opened the car door. "No, wait. I don't think anyone will look for this car," he said, pointing to the BMW. He threw the bags in the trunk while Cassandra ran back inside the house for the keys. When she returned, they jumped in and backed out of the garage. A remote control inside the Beamer shut the door after them.

He drove down the secluded road and within minutes, heard tires crunching on the gravel. "Son of a bitch," he screamed and pointed to headlights in the distance. "There they are."

Cassandra cried. Anthony made a wide turn down a service road and did a U-turn to face the main road. He turned the lights off on the car, but kept it idling, waiting for their escape. Sure enough, a large black van sped past headed toward the lake house.

"Who are they?" she breathed, as if they could hear her.

"I don't know," Anthony answered. "But, I don't plan on finding out." As soon as he knew the coast was clear, he put the car in drive and took off. He prayed the detour he set up would work for a little while.

"I let myself forget," Cassandra bawled. "Being at the lake house was like being on vacation. But, they're back and trying to kill me."

"Not gonna happen," Anthony said, and he meant it. They arrived at an abandoned warehouse and Cassandra glanced around as they pulled into a back alleyway. Anthony could see the disappointment in her face as if she thought Plan B would be nicer than the basement. He frowned when he thought about it. The boss discussed Plan B with him while he was still in prison. It wasn't anything luxurious, quite the opposite, and he knew the outcome would put a damper on their newfound relationship.

They each grabbed a bag, along with the pillows and blankets, and snuck into the building. Anthony flipped a switch but there wasn't any electricity. She stood close to him. Anthony found an office with a large broken window. It would provide a little light, just like the night before. He tried to smile, knowing they could get through this.

Cassandra shrugged. "Not as dirty as before," she said sarcastically as she ran her finger along the abandoned furniture. Living on the run had become her new way of life and she grew used to it.

Anthony admired her cooperation. She didn't fight or try to get away from him. She got it now, he thought to himself. He pulled her close and kissed her. "I'm hungry," he said as their mouths separated.

She laid blankets on the floor, then opened the fish container. The stench burned their noses, but they ate it anyway. It hadn't been more than a few hours since he cooked it. Anthony reached into the bag for a can of soda for them to share. He didn't know how long they'd be there and he wanted to make sure their supplies lasted.

After swallowing some food, he reached into his pocket for the flip phone and texted the boss. *We're safe in the warehouse.*
-Alright. I'll be in touch.-

Chapter 15

ONCE AGAIN, FEAR CONSUMED Cassandra's mind. The bad guys were hot on their heels and she knew it. She pushed her food around the paper plate and choked on her emotions. Anthony reached over and held her hand. Cassandra knew if it weren't for him, she'd go crazy. More than ever, she craved her medication, but understood why she couldn't have it. That girl was gone, somehow, she had changed, and it scared her shitless.

"Now what?" she asked in hopes of answers. He knew much more than she did, and yet she knew someone out there knew more than he did. It confused her.

"We wait," he answered.

Anthony laid on the blankets. Cassandra crawled toward him and nestled herself into his arms. She closed her eyes and could still smell the lake all over their skin. She remembered jumping back into the water, naked, after their sex ended. A smile stretched across her face.

He turned and faced her. His fingers traced her nose and trailed down her jawline. Anthony brushed the hair out of her eyes before he leaned over and kissed her. Heat filled Cassandra. There was no way she could lose her virginity and die in the same day, she thought. She now lived a nightmare, everything scared her, except him.

"You look pretty comfortable for a kidnapped girl," he joked.

He pulled her closer to him and she laughed. "If it makes you feel better," she suggested, "you can always tie me up." Cassandra giggled, but then stopped. She wondered how she could flirt when her life was on the line.

Anthony pushed her away and stood up. "You want it rough, huh?" He sounded harsh, but his grin gave him away.

"No. But, I am getting a little too comfy for a hostage."

"You're not a hostage, girl." His eyes sparkled in the moonlight as he spoke. "You're my slave. My sex-slave."

Cassandra blushed and batted her lashes. Excitement rushed through her bones at the thought. She licked her lips then blew him a kiss. Anthony rummaged through the abandoned office and when his laughter echoed through the room she wondered what he'd found.

He stood in front of her and pulled her to her feet. "What are you doing?"

Anthony held Cassandra's face and kissed her. His lips pressed hard into hers. His tongue jammed down her throat, almost choking her. She coughed, and he smiled. "Take your clothes off," Anthony demanded.

She sensed the authority in his voice but knew she wouldn't obey if he truly tortured her. "No," she said as she planted her feet on the floor and crossed her arms.

"What was that? Listen bitch," he couldn't control his laughter. "I said take your clothes off."

Cassandra stood still. He reached for the gun hoisted in his jeans and her clothes quickly fell off. He pulled her into him and unfastened her bra. His warm fingers gave her goosebumps. Cassandra slid her fingers between her flesh and the trim of her panties. Anthony's breath burned on her neck and the panties dropped. Cassandra stood naked, just like he requested.

Anthony pulled something out of his pocket. She couldn't see in the darkness, but a cloth of some sort covered her eyes. Her nipples stood erect. He took her hands and pulled them behind her. Anthony tied her wrists together, and the rope itched her already raw skin.

He licked her lips and she responded by opening her mouth. Cassandra felt his thumb move up her chin and into her mouth. It was salty, but she sucked it. Anthony pushed her to her knees and his clothing brushed against her as they fell to the floor.

His hand reached behind her head and held it in place. Anthony's dick rubbed against Cassandra's lips, and just like his thumb, she accepted it. He tilted her head back, "Open up as wide as you can," he instructed her.

She'd never done that before. As scary as it was, it thrilled her at the same time. Moisture built up between her legs as he thrust himself down her throat. Cassandra coughed for real. She tried to speak but couldn't.

His hands cupped her face and his stomach pressed against her nose. Tears dripped down onto his hands, and drool spilled out of her mouth. Cassandra choked on his erection, her breasts were so hard they hurt.

Anthony released her, and she took a deep breath. He yanked her elbows and forced her to stand and walk with him. He lowered Cassandra's torso onto the desk. "Spread your legs for me," he said.

Anthony adjusted her defenseless body. His finger slipped inside her folds, pulling her juices out. "Mmm," she moaned. He continued, in and out as she burned with desire. He didn't warn or tease her, but Anthony thrusted his large cock deep and fast. "Ouch," she cried out.

"I'm sorry," he whispered. "I forgot you're not used to this." He didn't let up, just inched further and further. Cassandra took another deep breath as the pain eased.

Anthony reached around and aroused her button. The room spun, and she felt lightheaded. Then, something amazing happened, her first orgasm. She felt his hand on her back. "Oh my God," she whimpered.

He wasn't finished yet. Anthony released himself from her and whipped off her blindfold. He spun her around and sat her on the desk. Her ass neared the edge. Cassandra feared falling off, but his strong arms held onto her.

Anthony dipped in again, slowly at first, then building speed. Her breast heaved in the excitement. Cassandra leaned against her fists. He pulled her waist into him and his explosion caused her body to shake.

Cassandra shivered as Anthony carried her over to the blanket and laid her down. She assumed it was over, but he remained between her shaky legs. After violently kissing her, Anthony lowered himself.

He kissed her inner thighs and scooted his hands beneath her, lifting her ass off the floor. He raised her vagina to his mouth. Anthony's tongue caressed every inch of her. She arched her back and felt herself come again.

They rested for a moment, but Anthony still hovered over her. Their breathing was the only sound in the room. Anthony adjusted himself and teased her with the head of his dick. "Please," she begged.

He pushed into Cassandra once again. Her legs wrapped around his back. They rocked back and forth for what seemed like an eternity until they both exploded and Anthony collapsed beside her. Cassandra tried to speak but the weight of the day, and the euphoria of their sex, caused her eyes to close. Sleep found them both.

Chapter 16

ANTHONY WOKE BEFORE Cassandra. Her naked body cuddled against his as he watched her chest rise and fall as she breathed. She looked fragile, which reminded him he had a job to do. Both their lives depended on him protecting her, and he set out to do that. Anthony slipped his arm out from under her and gently lowered Cassandra back onto the blankets.

He'd been as quiet as he could while dressing, but the sound of his zipper woke her. "Where are you going?" Cassandra sat up and rubbed her eyes.

Anthony slipped into his sneakers and hoisted the gun in his jeans. "I need to check out the property." He leaned over and kissed the top of her head. Cassandra trembled which caused him to harden, his anger not guided at her but toward those who wanted to hurt her. He turned to leave but knew he wouldn't have to lock her inside this time. Cassandra understood, which made his job a little easier. "Don't open this for anyone." She nodded, and he continued to walk outside.

Factories neighbored the warehouse. Anthony thought there would be more of a hustle in the morning, but it appeared none of them were operational. He saw nothing unusual and checked out the inside of the warehouse. As Anthony peered down hallways and searched other offices, the flip phone vibrated.

"Yeah," he answered, already knowing who the caller was.

The boss snapped. "You're surrounded. Get her out of there, now!"

"What?" Anthony replied. Sweat beads formed on his forehead as his heart pounded in his chest. "How did this happen?" The coast was clear just moments before, he thought.

"You! You dumb shit," the boss screamed. Anthony heard traffic in the background and knew if the boss was driving, then crap was getting real. "What the fuck were you thinking? You took the BMW?"

Anthony swallowed with guilt. "I wanted them to think she was on the property. Figured, with the old car there, they'd..." he stopped in mid-sentence. Holy fuck, he thought to himself, it was his fault. "There's a tracker installed, isn't there?" He ran his fingers through his hair as he recalled looking for flashing lights upon their arrival to the lake house. He didn't go through the interior of the car and wondered if the device hid in the glove box.

"Yes. And now he's there."

"He?" Anthony questioned the boss but knew who he spoke of.

The boss screamed as Anthony ran through the warehouse. He knew he fucked up. "Yes, he wants to make sure the job gets done this time. Our only hope is there are more exits than there are men. Find one they're not watching and send her here. Now!"

"I'm on it," he responded to the demand. He was about to flip the phone shut, but the sound of his boss saying something else, stopped him.

"He assumes you're the one responsible for hiding Cassandra. The Feds are on their way, too. He will pin this murder on you. He's prepared to say you escaped to finish what you left behind all those years ago."

Anthony backed into a wall and brought his fist down as hard as he could. "There will be no murder," he shouted into the phone and flipped it shut. In the distance, he heard a feminine scream. Anthony took off again and prayed he could get to her in time.

Chapter 17

CASSANDRA STRAIGHTENED out the blankets and pillows. They were hiding in an awful place, but she grew used to it. The sun shone through the window and onto the desk. Her nipples stood erect thinking of what he did to her on it. The room wasn't as bad as the basement hideout, and she didn't mind being there with him if she remained his sex-slave.

Her back was toward the door when she heard it open. Tiny hairs on the back of her neck stood up, and she didn't understand why. She heard footsteps headed her way and assumed the perimeter checked out. "I hear you baby," she whispered seductively.

"Where is the son-of-a-bitch?"

Cassandra's father stood before her. All fears of dying faded, thinking he would send her off to a safe place and have his security team watch over her. "Daddy, thank God you're here." She realized he would assume Anthony was out to hurt her, and needed to explain before anything happened. "This isn't what it looks like."

He didn't embrace her and the hairs on her neck rose again. Cassandra's instincts told her something was wrong as he stepped closer to her. The cold nose of a gun pressed into the side of her head.

"Daddy?" She bawled. "What are you doing?"

"I always hated when you called me that," he growled.

Do you realize what you've done? Anthony's words echoed in her head. Everything made sense, Anthony's anger when she attempted to call her father, not once but twice. She wondered why Anthony never told her who the real killer was, not that she would have believed him.

Cassandra couldn't breathe. Her father couldn't have killed her mother, her memory recalled he was out of town on business that night. She squeezed her eyes shut, expecting to die at any moment, but he hadn't pulled the trigger. Yet.

"I should have done this long ago. If you didn't escape, you would have died the same night as your mother. She was nothing but a whore." William Frame watched her pop her eyes open and then he followed them down to the makeshift bed on the floor. "Looks like the apple didn't fall too far from the tree." He paused and shuffled his feet to get a better stance. "You're not my daughter, Cassandra. She tried to hide that from me, but I found out."

Cassandra needed to be braver than she'd ever had. Even when Anthony portrayed himself as an abductor, she always sensed the good in him. Her father didn't give her the same impression. He raised her, she thought. Even if what he said was true, he must have loved her. "You killed Mama?"

"Shut up," his voice growled harsher than Anthony's ever did. "I didn't do it myself, and you got away. I can't have the same mistake happen again."

"Why?" she cried, trying to buy herself time. "That was fifteen years ago. Why do you want me dead now?"

Cassandra dared to look in his direction. She wanted to believe he would not hurt her. "Now?" he mocked. "I planned this for years. I've always wanted you dead. When you got away that fateful night, I had to act like I cared. Oh, my poor baby girl," he taunted. "Thank God she's safe."

Cassandra shook her head in disbelief. Her mouth opened to speak, but no sounds came out.

"If anyone killed you shortly after, it would have set off red flags. I have a business and reputation to withhold. So, I sent you away as often as I could. Now you've inherited your grandmother's millions." Cassandra's eyes widened. The inheritance wasn't a surprise, knowing he wanted the money more than her, was. "Now it's time for you to die."

The gun pressed further into her skull and she closed her eyes. Instead of hearing the trigger, Cassandra heard a loud thud and heard the gun hit the floor. Cassandra opened her eyes and found Anthony standing over her father's body. "Is he dead?" she cried hysterically as she noticed the bloody brick in Anthony's hand.

Anthony shook his head. "No, I told you I'm not a murderer." He pulled her close and pulled her a safe distance from William, just in case the older man woke up. Her hands shook as they wrapped around his neck. Anthony lifted her chin and looked her in the eyes. Cassandra trembled as she noticed his blue eyes pool up with tears and she knew the danger wasn't over.

Cassandra took a step back "I'm not strong enough for this," she cried as he lifted her chin to give her instructions.

"You need to get out of here as fast as you can, Cassandra."

"Not without you." She leaned in to kiss his cheek. Anthony held her at bay and tears blurred her vision.

He looked down at her father. "He's not the only one here. They're all here, and it's you they're after." Cassandra reached for his waist and hung on tight. Anthony pushed her away. "Run, Cassandra, out of the door and take a right. Run as fast as you can down to the end of the hall. There's an exit there, the only one they can't see. Go straight, don't look back, cross the bridge and turn left towards the overpass. You'll see a yellow Mustang. Get inside."

"No," she protested again. "Not without you."

He pulled her to the door as the man who raised her as his own stirred. "Trust me," he urged her to go, but she didn't budge. "I love you, Cassandra, now run!" Anthony pushed her out the door.

Cassandra had no choice but to do what he said. The sun blinded her as she exited the building. She shielded her head as she ran as fast as she could and prayed she remembered the correct directions. After crossing the bridge, she was unsure which way he told her to turn.

Run, Cassandra, run. Her mother's words haunted her. She kept repeating them in her head until she said them, too.

CASSANDRA'S LEGS WERE like jelly and she stumbled a few times. In the distance, she saw the car, just like Anthony said. She prayed for safety. It could have been a setup, she imagined, and maybe this was how she would die.

The memory of his kisses gave her strength. She trusted him and knew Anthony wouldn't send her away to her death. A warmth spread through her like wildfire as she remembered her protector telling her he loved her. She didn't have time to say it in return.

The Mustang's passenger door opened and she raced toward it and jumped inside when she arrived. The door slammed shut and Cassandra hid her head between her knees. A gentle hand rubbed her back, and she jumped.

"Governor Johnson?" Her mother's dear friend sat beside her. He had been a family friend long before Cassandra's birth. "You're the one responsible for saving me?"

"You're safe now, Cassandra." The governor rested his hand on her shoulder to calm her.

A half smile formed across his face. Cassandra studied him, his hair color, his nose and jawline. She'd never looked at him like that before. She saw herself in his image and wondered why she'd never picked up on that before. Her breathing slowed down, but her sobs were out of control. "Are you my..." Cassandra choked on the emotions that raged through her. "My..." she couldn't say the words.

He nodded. "It would have put you at great risk to tell you. I didn't know until a few years ago." She cried as he continued with the story. "One day I felt lost without your mother around, and I looked at some things she left at my house. There was a note from her, dated the night she died, telling me about you. I put the pieces together and checked into William. He's been planning your death for years, and I've been planning your safety."

Cassandra leaned back onto the seat and rubbed her eyes. Her mother saved her life, her true protector. She shuddered to think what could have happened if the governor never saw the note. He reached over and took her hand. Governor Johnson had been there for her many times since her mother died. William must have kept up with the charade to allow him to be there when she graduated and when her grandmother passed away, along with many other times. Unless, Cassandra thought, the man who raised her didn't know the identity of her biological father. Cassandra felt comforted, but only for a while.

She looked ahead out of the windshield. The warehouse stood in the distance below them. She glanced at the governor and wondered if he thought the same thing as her. "We need to get Anthony," she told him.

"Can't now." He frowned. "The police and Feds are already on their way." She looked his way with puzzled brows. "William called them, figured out who was behind your supposed abduction and used it to his advantage."

"No," she screamed and reached to open the car door. Governor Johnson pulled her away from it. "They'll take him back to prison."

He held her shoulder and looked in her eyes. "Has anything gone on with you two?"

"Yes." Cassandra wasn't afraid to tell him the truth. She thought she once heard Anthony mumble something to himself about her being forbidden to him, but she wasn't afraid to admit the truth. "Please don't punish him," she begged. "The feelings were mutual."

To her surprise, the governor didn't seem upset. "I suppose those things are natural to young people like yourself." He cocked a half grin and looked away from her when speaking. "I knew he'd do the opposite of what I told him." He started the car but didn't put it in gear. "I promised to pardon him, Cassandra, and I don't break promises. You have to trust me."

Cassandra sensed something horrible. Before she could say anything to him, he reached over to protect her as a loud blast caused the road to rumble. She looked up to see the warehouse explode, flames were shooting out the windows and rooftop. "Anthony," she hollered.

Chapter 18

THE GOVERNOR DROVE with caution toward the warehouse. Sirens blared around them. He pulled to the right as firetrucks whipped by. "We can't get any closer," he told her. They were about two blocks away from the fire.

Cassandra jumped out of the car and ran. The governor huffed as he caught up and grabbed her arm. "I need to get to him," she cried.

"What you need to do is play the victim. Can you do that?"

She nodded and lowered her pace. Cassandra didn't need to play, she was the victim. Together, they walked up the yellow crime tape. She attempted to limbo beneath it, but a strong hand stopped her.

"Nobody behind the line," a voice of authority demanded. The officer looked at them and lowered his head in shame. "I'm sorry, Governor Johnson, we weren't expecting you." He glanced at her and raised the tape for them to follow him. "Cassandra Frame? We assumed you were in the building. I'm glad you're alright."

The officer walked them over to an ambulance and told the paramedics who she was. They forced her to sit still and examined her body. He radioed the Chief of Police. "Sir, the girl is alive." Within minutes swarms of officers and the chief surrounded her.

The Chief questioned Cassandra. "Do you know who abducted you?"

"No, sir," she answered. She didn't know who was behind the farce until a few minutes prior.

"How did you escape?" Another officer asked while writing it all down in a little notebook.

She held her hands up as she talked, bullshit fell from her mouth. "I finished loosening the rope he had me tied up with," the brush burn from their rough sex made them believe her. "I heard a commotion, like a fight of some sort, and used that time to my advantage."

"And you, Governor, what are you doing here?"

The governor noticed the bruises on Cassandra's body for the first time. He stared at them as he spoke. Cassandra sensed his anger. She wanted to tell him she was fine, but she couldn't just yet. "The Frames and I have been close friends for years, longer than this young girl has lived. William called me in a panic. He said something happened to Cassandra and he needed help. I found her running for her life about a half mile up the road when I arrived just a few minutes ago."

It all sounded realistic. Part of her beamed knowing she would be safe, but knowing Anthony was out there unprotected terrorized her. The firefighters were trying to contain the burning building. Anthony couldn't be inside, she told herself and gulped in fear.

The Chief put his hand on her shoulder, it startled her. He apologized. "There is nothing to fear. The man who did this to you is dead. He'll never hurt you again."

She tried her hardest not to cry. She wasn't supposed to be in love with the man who took her away from the life she knew. Cassandra felt shocked and couldn't speak. The governor asked, "Are there any survivors?"

"No, Sir," the officer in charge responded, as he held his hat in his hand.

Cassandra's head snapped in their direction. She wanted to hear the words, needed them to tell her the real man who tried to hurt her died himself. "Nobody?" she quivered. They expected her to cry this time, but her tears weren't for her father.

"I'm sorry," he looked down as he spoke. "Your father, William Frame is one of the confirmed deceased."

She broke down and bawled her eyes out. Governor Johnson wrapped his arm around her. All she could think about was not getting the chance to tell Anthony she loved him. "What am I going to do?" The air was thick, and Cassandra couldn't breathe.

"You'll survive," the governor said. She looked up to the eyes that matched hers and heard the irony in his voice. He touched the scrapes on her arm and ran his finger to rope burn on her wrists. "I'm sorry this happened to you."

Chapter 19

CASSANDRA STOOD AMONG friends and family under an overcast sky. The priest chanted prayers as she looked down at the opening in the ground. Her tears were sincere. Cassandra loved him, before she knew his true colors, like a daughter should. Her emotions clustered in confusion, he didn't love her.

She stood tall and acted brave once again. William's secrets would remain hidden. There wasn't a need to tell people how wicked he was. Cassandra's life would go on.

Her eyes watched intently as his casket was lowered into the ground. Governor Johnson nudged her elbow. Cassandra walked up to the casket, and the white rose she'd been holding fell. She paused in silence for a moment. Everyone watched her, waiting for her to say something but she didn't. Cassandra turned around and fell into the governor's arms. The crowd sobbed for her, but only he knew why she mourned.

The crowd took their turns paying their last respects to William, one by one, then left her standing there. Governor Johnson stood by her side, but she refused to leave. She wanted to watch them bury the man who died trying to kill her. Strong men shoveled dirt and tossed it on the coffin. When they finished, she finally turned to leave.

At the house, people gathered around her. She wondered if they came for her, or the food and drinks, the house was packed like a nightclub. One by one, they told Cassandra how sorry they were for her. She wanted to scold them, tell them she would be better off with 'her father' gone, but refrained.

She felt skeptical as she looked around at their faces, wondering if they were all evil villains, plotting her death. Or, were they victims like herself? Dr. Allen Jenson sat beside her. "I think you need to talk about this. Come to the office in the morning." Cassandra said nothing to him, just walked away and avoided him for the rest of the afternoon. It hurt her to think someone who'd been so caring toward her for years, had just been putting on an act. Cassandra had no intentions on talking to him ever again.

She sat in the corner and planned her life. There wasn't any point in staying there, to be reminded day after day how William planned to kill her for fifteen years.

Cassandra looked to Governor Johnson from across the room. His eyes met hers and he nodded. He understood her more than she ever thought. Sunlight faded from the windows and at last she found herself alone. The funeral traditions were over.

Memories of Anthony flooded her mind. She held onto her broken heart. Cassandra turned on the television and listened to the news reports.

"Authorities tell us that Anthony Flint's death is confirmed. The felon abducted Cassandra Frame after his escape from the state penitentiary two weeks ago. Witnesses say he held the girl for ransom and planned on using the money to leave the country. William Frame met with Flint in an abandoned warehouse in hopes to see his daughter released safely. Both Frame and Flint

were killed in a fiery explosion. Cassandra Frame is home and doing well."

She threw her glass of water at the screen and screamed. The governor explained that honoring William, and blaming Anthony was for the best, but she didn't like it. Anthony gave his life saving hers, he deserved recognition. Cassandra cupped her face and sniffled. She decided to stop crying and to carry on, the way Anthony would want her too.

Chapter 20

CASSANDRA LISTENED to the family attorney read the Last Will and Testament. William kept her in it, leaving his billions and business to her. She assumed he planned on changing it after her death, after taking her Grandmother's millions, if his plan succeeded.

The attorney shook her hand. "Again," he said, "my condolences on your loss." Cassandra nodded and accepted his kind words. "Do you have any plans?"

She shook her head. "I need time to figure things out," she told him, being as sincere as she could be. William ran a successful business, but she wasn't interested in it. Cassandra planned to sell it but said nothing, figuring the attorney didn't need to know. She was sure he'd been on William's dirty payroll. When the time came to sell, Cassandra didn't plan on using his services.

He walked her to the door and placed his hand over her shoulder. Cassandra flinched, not trusting anyone any longer. "If you need anything, just call me," he told her as she entered the elevator.

Cassandra turned her head toward him. "Thank you."

THE GOVERNOR DROVE her to William's private airport. It looked nothing like commercial airports she used every time he shipped her off to Europe. There was only one building, a tower, and a runway with a jet idling on it, waiting for her. Her jet now, she laughed to herself. She decided to leave the country. After years of posh boarding schools, this seemed the most natural for her.

Cassandra smiled, her true friends scattered across the world and she wanted to see them. America didn't hold much for her. She knew where she came from, and planned on returning from time to time, but she would enjoy her life on foreign shores.

The governor glanced at her and read her mind. "You'll always have me," he smiled.

Cassandra reached over and touched his hand. He'd been there for her more times than she could count. "I owe you my life, for fuck's sake," not afraid to let her new-self speak. "I'll stay in touch," she assured him. He looked at her and she knew he wanted to say something. Cassandra shook her head to stop him. "You've had years to come to terms with this parenting thing. I just found out weeks ago, and it will take time."

He nodded in agreement. They stepped out of the car and he took her luggage out of the trunk. Cassandra stood still, looking at the jet. New adventures and a lifetime of happiness awaited her.

The governor handed her suitcases over to the pilot. The pilot looked in her direction and she nodded. He was a good guy, hired by Cassandra herself. Anyone who worked for William were all suspicious to her. He tossed her things into a cargo area and brushed his hands together. "I'm ready whenever you are," he said. "Just buzz when you want to take off." He climbed up into the plane and took a left to the cockpit.

"I'll expect postcards," the Governor instructed. He embraced her and for the first time in a long time, Cassandra felt loved.

"Of course." She kissed him on the cheek. "I've given up all social media, so postcards and phone calls are all you'll have." He looked concerned, and she hugged him again. "And of course, we'll see each other often. I can't thank you enough for all you've done for me."

He let go of Cassandra and she walked up the stairs. The interior of the jet had luxury designed all over, but it all paled when she saw blue. Blue eyes.

Anthony sat there, waiting for her. She screamed with disbelief and ran to him. Anthony stood and wrapped his arms around her. Cassandra squeezed him tight, like she'd never wanted to let go. "I didn't want to believe you died in that explosion." Tears of joy escaped her eyes, but Cassandra didn't try to wipe them away.

He cupped her face and kissed her, more tender than he ever had before. Her heart raced, and her knees wobbled. "I'm sorry we couldn't tell you what plan B was. We knew it was a risk and I could have died, but we were able to fake my death. I'll never leave you again."

Cassandra pressed into him and rubbed her hands up and down his body. He was rock hard beneath his tight leather pants. Cassandra's lips opened wide and persuaded him to enter. Anthony pulled back. "Not on the plane," he told her. "We have our whole lives ahead of us."

They took their seats and fastened their seatbelts. Cassandra looked out the window. Her real father stood there looking lost already. "Thank you," she mouthed again. Without him, she wouldn't have been hidden, William's secrets wouldn't ruin her name, and Anthony wouldn't have been given a second chance at life.

Anthony reached for Cassandra's chin and turned her face toward him. His eyes sparkled as his smile spread across his face. The entire world thought he died in a fierce explosion. Thanks to the boss he had a new identification. Cassandra breathed easy knowing they'd never try to take her man away again.

"I love you too," she said to him. He tilted his head and she read his mind. "It was the last thing you said that day." She grinned. "I never had the chance to say it back."

"Hmm." He laughed. "Tell me again." He kissed her. "And, again, and again."

Cassandra let the pilot know they were ready for takeoff, then pulled Anthony's head toward her. "I love you Anthony, um..." she paused, "I mean, Andrew."

The jet raced down the runway and they ascended into the clouds. Anthony held her hand next to his heart. "I love you, too." Cassandra reached over and brushed her hands through his hair as she kissed him all over his face and neck. Their new life together had only just begun.

Join Friends of Florella Newsletter

TO BE NOTIFIED FOR upcoming releases and author alerts: please sign up for my newsletter.

Click here to join[1]

---

1. https://www.subscribepage.com/r0z9b9

Follow Florella Grant

<u>OFFICIAL WEBSITE</u> [1]
 <u>Facebook</u>[2]
 <u>Twitter</u>[3]
 <u>InstaGram</u>[4]
 <u>GoodReads</u>[5]
 <u>Join Friends of Florella Reading Group</u>[6]

Other books by Florella Grant

Hitched While Intoxicated[7] (Contemporary Romance. Mild steam level)

Love At 320 Sycamore[8] (Contemporary Romance. Second Chance. Short story/novelette. Sweet read.)

---

1. https://www.florellagrant.com/

2.   https://www.facebook.com/florellagrant

3.   https://www.twitter.com/florellagrant

4.   https://www.instagram.com/florellagrant73

5.   https://www.goodreads.com/florellagrant73

6.   https://www.facebook.com/groups/friendsofflorellagrant/

7.   **https://www.books2read.com/u/47Zg9A**

8.   **https://www.books2read.com/u/m0x5dl**

Don't miss out!

Visit the website below and you can sign up to receive emails whenever Florella Grant publishes a new book. There's no charge and no obligation.

https://books2read.com/r/B-A-IVDF-DXCT

BOOKS 2 READ

Connecting independent readers to independent writers.

Also by Florella Grant

Hidden

Watch for more at www.florellagrant.com.